Blame It On The Secret Santa

Samantha Baca

Sugarplum Falls Series

Blame It On The Mistletoe

Blame It On The Eggnog

Blame It On The Candy Canes

Blame It On The Blizzard

Blame It On The Reindeer

Blame It On The Carols

Blame It On The Lattes

Blame It On The Secret Santa

Copyright © 2024 by Samantha Baca.

All rights reserved. If you are reading this book and did not purchase it, this book has been pirated, and you are stealing. Please delete it from your device and support the author by purchasing a legal copy.
All rights reserved. No part of this book may be reproduced or transmitted in any form or by any means, electronic or mechanical, including photocopying, recording, or by information storage and retrieval system, without written permission of the publisher, except where permitted by law. This book is a work of fiction. Names, places, characters, and incidents are the product of the author's imagination or are used fictitiously.

Cover Design: Richard Baca
Image (s): DepositPhotos

Contents

<u>One</u>
Cassidy

"You've got to be kidding me," I mumbled, staring at the small, folded piece of paper in my hands. Bruce, our manager, went on about the Secret Santa gift exchange while the bowl of names was passed around the breakroom as everyone took one. It wasn't that I was grumpy about doing a gift exchange—we did one every year. It was that I *hated* the person who I drew, and from the way he had acted toward me since he started working at Waldon's, I was sure he hated me, too.

My eyes scanned the room until I found fucker face's head. His short brown hair fell in a messy heap, but what was even more infuriating was how it looked perfectly tousled, just like it used to when I would run my fingers through it. Blue eyes looked up and caught mine, so I quickly looked away after making sure to give him an ice-cold glare first.

Sean had been working for Waldon's for three months, but I had known him since we were five years old and in kindergarten together. Back then, he was nice. He helped me when I fell off the monkey bars and got me a band-aid from the nurse when I scraped my knee. We were friends through most of our childhood years until we became teenagers and made the mistake of dating in eleventh grade. That lasted a whole six months until a rumor spread around the school and ended things for us on the spot. Since then, I hadn't stopped despising Sean Wheeler.

Bruce finished up the meeting after going on and on about this being the jolliest time of year and how our smiles can speak a thousand words. Basically, this translated to—you work retail and it's going to be a busy, grueling three weeks while everyone tries to cram all of their Christmas shopping into one trip—so don't be grumpy about it.

I got up and headed to the sales floor so I could get as far away from Sean as possible. It was bad enough that I had drawn his name for the gift exchange, but I didn't want to get stuck working with him today, either.

"Hey, slow down," Rachel said, rushing to keep up with me. She was the only one at Waldon's I had really considered to be my friend, mainly because we were the same age and had gone to school together. Everyone else was either of retirement age or still in high school.

"Sorry, I was just trying to get to the sporting goods department before fucker face could beat me," I said, glancing over my shoulder to see where Sean had gone. Rachel chuckled, fully knowing our history and how much I disliked our coworker.

"It doesn't matter. Bruce started assignments this morning, so we don't get to decide which department we want to work in anymore. You and I are both in toys today."

I tossed my head back and groaned. The toy department was the *worst* department to be in any time after Thanksgiving. It didn't matter what day it was or what time of day—parents would come flocking in, desperate to get their hands on a sold-out toy that they couldn't find anywhere else. Even when we gave them dates for when we would get our next shipment, they still demanded that we go in the back and check, just to be sure we didn't have one hiding on the shelves.

"Don't seem so happy to be stuck with me today," she teased, pinning her Waldon employee nametag to her shirt.

"I hate toys," I moaned, looking at her as I put mine on.

"I know. But we'll make today fun. Maybe it won't be as busy."

"It's a Saturday and three weeks until Christmas. We'll be lucky if we have time to stop and pee, let alone eat lunch today," I replied, not hiding the dread in my tone. I wasn't trying to take my bad mood out on Rachel, but drawing Sean's name in the gift exchange was literally the worst thing that could happen to me.

"I love your positive, cheery attitude," she teased, giving me an exaggerated smile as she made fun of the pep talk Bruce had just given. "Don't forget to smile and show the world how much Christmas joy we have to give at Waldon's."

"How about we take that Christmas joy and shove it right up Sean's as—"

"Right up my what?" Sean asked, coming from out of nowhere and startling me. He rocked back on his heels and shoved his hands in his pockets as he smirked at me. *I hated that smirk.*

Of course he was there. Why wouldn't he be? It would be impossible for him to fully irritate me if he weren't always around.

"Well, since you were eavesdropping, I was gonna say right up your ass."

Why bother lying when he clearly knows how I feel about him? It had been over twelve years, and my feelings for him hadn't changed one bit. My grudge against Sean was something I would surely take to the grave.

"Aww, that's not really the way you want to talk about the person who is responsible for bringing you some extra holiday cheer this year, is it?"

I narrowed my eyes and glared at him. What was he talking about?

"You know, the whole *Secret Santa* thing," he whispered loudly, pretending to look around to make sure no one heard him. My heart sank as my stomach soured.

"You've got to be kidding me," I groaned. "You drew my name?"

"I sure did. And while I know it's supposed to be a secret, I figured I'd let you in on it since you were talking so nicely about me before you knew I was there."

"You can do what you want," I said with a shrug. "There's nothing that's going to change how I feel about you." I gave him the fakest smile I had and stared him down until he broke eye contact.

"Well, then. Let the games begin." He winked, and it sent chills over my skin in the worst way.

"What's that supposed to mean?" I demanded with my hands planted firmly on my hips.

"You'll see." He walked off, tossing the words carelessly over his shoulder. Ugh. He seriously got under my skin just by breathing.

"Seriously—what is that supposed to mean? What games?"

I balled my fists at my sides and growled in frustration that he hadn't answered me.

"Ugh. He is the worst." I shook my head and tried to take a deep, calming breath as Rachel grinned at me. "What? What's that smile about?"

"Nothing. I just see a romance in the making. That's all."

I pulled my head back and scrunched my face in disgust.

"Are you kidding me? Do you not remember us dating in high school and what a cluster fuck that was? Dating Sean is the *last* thing I would ever do."

"Have you never heard of enemies to lovers and second chance romance?"

"No. But I have heard of enemies who do everything they can to kill the person who drives them crazy." I held my hands in front of me and mimicked choking Sean.

She rolled her eyes and headed to the customer service station where she and I would be working today. Each department had one to keep the line down at the main customer service desk, which was used for returning items and answering general questions. It was pretty basic, with two computers so we could look up inventory when needed.

"So what? He got your name in the drawing. It's not that bad."

"It's terrible. Not only did he draw *my* name, *I* had the unfortunate luck of drawing *his*."

Rachel's eyes widened nearly as big as her smile.

"Stop it," I hissed, pointing a finger at her as I glared. "Whatever love spell you're trying to conjure up inside of that hopeless romantic head of yours isn't going to work. Sean is the enemy and it's imperative that you remember that."

She could believe in fairy tales and happily ever after all she wanted, but one thing I knew for sure was that Sean and I would never, ever get back together.

Two
Sean

My head was throbbing by the time lunch came around, not that there was time to actually take a lunch break. I was stuck up front working a register but couldn't stop thinking about getting Cassidy's name in the gift exchange. How weird was it that I would pick her name out of the eighty-plus employees who worked at Waldon's? I knew she was mad when I first started working there, but this would royally piss her off knowing that *I* was the one getting her a gift for Christmas this year.

By the time my shift ended, I packed up my stuff and made my escape before Bruce could ask me to stay longer. I knew it was insanely busy today, and they needed the help, but there was also a limit to how much more I could take. Customer service was never my strong suit as I generally preferred to keep to myself and not have to talk to people if I didn't really have to—which was basically the opposite of what I was expected to do at Waldon's. It wasn't that I wanted to work there; I just didn't have many options at the time. I wasn't expecting to come back to Sugarplum Falls after being gone for twelve years, but when my mom called, saying she needed help, I made that my priority.

I pulled into the garage and turned off the car. My stomach growled, but I hadn't felt like stopping for fast food, even though it was quick and easy. I was doing my best to take care of myself, which meant eating right. I waited for the garage door to finish closing before opening the door into the house.

Just as I expected, waiting eagerly for me on the other side was Max, my incredibly needy and overly attached Doberman Pinscher.

"Hey, Max. I told you I would be back," I said, scratching his head as he jumped up and put two paws on my chest. I looked around and chuckled when I saw all of the throw pillows from the couch had been tossed to the floor, and a box of tissue had been shredded to pieces.

"We really gotta work on your anxiety." I continued to rub his head for a few seconds before gently pushing him away so I could go set my stuff down.

He followed my every step, as was our daily routine since the day I adopted him a few years ago. His owner claimed he was defective because he had zero protective instincts and was too much of a wimp to be a guard dog. I immediately fell in love with him and could relate to not living up to society's opinions of what they expected you to be.

I grabbed the stuff from the fridge to make fajitas and fixed dinner while Max lay on the rug beside me. My phone rang, so I pulled it out of my pocket and smiled when I saw my mother's name on the screen.

"Hey, Mom," I said as I flipped the chicken in the skillet and turned down the heat.

"Hi, sweetie. How was work today?"

"Busy, but fine."

"I've heard so many wonderful things about you around town. Everyone is so happy to have you back."

"Not everyone," I mumbled under my breath as I piled the chicken in a tortilla.

"What was that dear? I couldn't hear you."

"Nothing," I lied, stepping over Max to get some salsa from the fridge. "What's up?"

"Well, I was calling to let you know that I talked to your brother, and he's going to come in for Christmas. I thought we could all sit down and have lunch together before…"

Her voice trailed off, and I knew what it was she wasn't saying. I hadn't talked to Declan, my twin brother, in over twelve years. Not since he'd been caught cheating on his girlfriend, but to get out of it, he lied and said it was me. This was the rumor that had immediately ended my relationship with Cassidy, and nothing I said or did could get her to hear me out. In her mind, I had been the one who was caught cheating, and she had never forgiven me.

I shoved a hand through my hair and sighed heavily.

"Yeah. That sounds great, Mom. Just let me know when, and I'll make sure to request the time off from work if I can."

"I don't want to make things harder for you, especially with all you're doing for us. If you want to send me the days that you have off, I could plan around those."

"Sure. I'll do that when we hang up."

"Thank you, son. I know things between you and your brother haven't been good for a while, but I'm hoping that with everything going on, you can both push those differences aside. I'd love at least one last wonderful Christmas with your dad while we still can."

I swallowed past the lump in my throat and nodded, even though she couldn't see me.

"I agree, Mom. We'll make this the best Christmas for him. For all of us."

We hung up after saying we loved each other, but I couldn't shake the overwhelming emotion that had been sitting on my shoulders since I'd first gotten the call about my dad.

After noticing several changes in him over a few months, my mother took him to the doctor to get checked out. They found that he had early-onset dementia, and unfortunately, he seemed to be progressing quickly. My mom was concerned about their finances due to him forgetting to pay several bills and falling behind. I agreed to come home and help them get caught up while she focused on his health and what the next steps would look like for them. But for now, our main focus was to make sure that we kept as much of our Christmas traditions as possible—even if that meant I had to suck it up and pretend to like my brother again.

Three
Cassidy

"Thank you. Have a great day," I said, forcing a smile as I passed a customer on my way out to collect the shopping carts from the corral. I wrapped my scarf tighter around my neck as I shivered against the brutal cold wind that whipped past.

Sugarplum Falls was about to get hit with another snowstorm, and this one was even worse than the one we had last week. It wasn't uncommon to get a lot of snow here, but these storms seemed to be bigger and stronger than anything we'd seen in over a decade, with record numbers reported by the meteorologist.

I hurried through the parking lot, covering my face with my hand to shield it from the snow blowing directly at me. I tried to take a deep breath, but the wind felt like it was suffocating me, making it hard to breathe.

"Why are you out here?" a deep voice asked as strong hands spun me around, and a tall, muscular body shielded me from the storm.

I narrowed my eyes and glared at him.

"How is that any of your business?" I questioned through chattering teeth. I tried to force my body to act calm so he couldn't see just how badly I was shivering. It was literally bone-chilling cold.

"It's *my* business because *you* have no business being out here."

"It's part of the job. Now move out of my way so I can do it and get back inside where it's warm and I won't lose a limb to frostbite."

"No."

I pulled my head back and deepened my glare.

"No?"

"That's right. I said no. You can fight me all you want, Cassidy, but there's no way in hell I'm allowing you to stay out here and gather shopping carts."

"Yeah, well, I hate to break it to you, but you're not my boss. So if you don't mind—"

"Hey, Bruce," Sean called, yelling over my head with a voice so boisterous it could be heard across the parking lot and over the howling wind. Even though it was impressive, I didn't dare let him see it.

"What's up?" Bruce asked, trotting over, bundled up in his winter jacket and scarf.

"I'd like to take over gathering the carts. Is it okay if Cassidy takes my spot at the register?"

Bruce looked between us, probably wondering what the real issue was.

I rolled my eyes and looked to the side, too pissed off at Sean to be able to think straight.

"Sure. That's fine. I'm just getting back from lunch, so I'll stay and help you get the carts, Sean. Go ahead and head back inside, Cassidy."

The inside of my cheek hurt from how hard I was biting it to keep quiet. I stormed off, heading back inside when I had to jerk to a stop at the last minute for a car that was going too fast for the sheet of ice they were driving on. I jumped out of the way to avoid being hit, but not before losing my balance and landing hard on my ass.

Four
Sean

I couldn't remember the last time I went ice skating, but I was impressed by both my speed and agility as I slid across the parking lot to get to Cassidy. I hadn't seen much of what happened until I heard the sound of brakes squealing as a car tried to avoid hitting her.

"Hey, are you okay?" I asked, immediately dropping to my knees as my eyes scanned her body, looking for any signs of injuries.

"Go away," she grunted, swatting my hand away as I tried to help her up.

"Stop being so damn difficult, Cassidy," I scolded, keeping my hands close by in case she lost her balance as she tried to stand up.

Bruce rushed over as well and tended to the old man in the car who had hit the steering wheel because of the force it took for the car to stop. He looked too old to be driving if you asked me, but that wasn't my concern right now. Cassidy was.

She stood beside me for a few minutes and winced every time she tried to take a step. Bruce was on his phone when he came over to check on her.

"Are you okay, Cassidy?" he asked, concern heavy on his face.

"Yeah. I think so."

"She can't walk," I blurted out, feeling the heat of her glare as she turned her face toward me. "I can take her to the hospital if you want."

Bruce nodded, looking back at the car and then at Cassidy.

"They're sending an ambulance for Jack, but I don't know how long it'll be before they can send a second one. If you don't mind taking her to get checked out, I'd greatly appreciate it."

"Not a problem at all." A wave of relief washed over me, not only that Cassidy appeared to be okay, but that I was going to get to take her to the hospital to make sure she was.

I knew it was pointless to talk to Cassidy right now, so I went and got my car, making sure to park as close to her as possible to make it easier for her to get in. I could tell it was painful for her to walk, and I knew it would also hurt trying to sit, but unless she laid across the backseat, there weren't any other options besides waiting for another ambulance.

"I can help you in," I offered as I came around the car and reached for her.

"No way in hell. I'm not going anywhere with you," she said with a bit too much hostility.

"You don't have much of a choice. It's clear that you're injured, so unless you want to stand outside and freeze your ass off until another ambulance can get out here, I'm your best option."

"It's a sad day in the world when *you* are the best option."

I took a deep breath and held it, refusing to let her attitude get to me.

"Alright, looks like you guys are set. Do you need help getting in, Cassidy?" Bruce asked, completely missing the pissed-off look on her face or the verbal exchange happening between us.

She looked away and shook her head.

"I'm fine. I don't need to go to the hospital," she insisted to Bruce.

"I would feel a lot better if you did. That was a nasty fall you had. The company will pay for everything if that's what you're worried about. I'll also pay both of you for the rest of the day so you don't miss any hours."

"That's not the issue. I'm fine. Really. I just want to go back inside and finish my shift."

"Let's see you walk then," I challenged, folding my arms over my chest. I knew this would only further irritate and piss her off, but I wasn't going to back down. She needed to go to the hospital to make sure she didn't break anything when she fell, and I wasn't going to stop until that happened. Cassidy was stubborn, but that was one of the things I had always loved about her. Until now.

Her eyes narrowed further at me as Bruce waited.

Cassidy pulled her shoulders back and went to take a step before hissing and freezing in pain.

"Exactly what I thought. Now you can either get in the car on your own, or I'll gladly help you inside," I said firmly, ignoring the smirk begging to cross Bruce's face. He knew our history the same as everyone else in Sugarplum Falls, so it wasn't like it was a big surprise to him how much she despised me.

"You're such a pain in my ass," Cassidy said through gritted teeth.

"No, I think the pain in your ass is from hitting the ice so hard. But thankfully, we're heading to a hospital with well-trained doctors who can confirm and prescribe some painkillers."

Cassidy allowed Bruce to help her in the backseat of my car and then continued to give me dirty looks all the way to the hospital.

Five
Cassidy

"Can you go somewhere else?" I practically snarled, hating that the nurse in the ER had allowed Sean to come back with me. There were long curtains that separated each of the beds, but he was sitting in the chair right beside me. If I had enough strength left in me, I'd find a way to make it where *he* was in one of the other beds instead.

"Sorry. No can do. The nurse said for me to sit here, so that's what I'm doing."

"She didn't say you *have* to sit there. She said you *could*. There's a big difference."

"Yeah, and I took her invite."

"But now *I'm* uninviting you."

Before we could continue with our bickering, the curtain pulled back, and an older man with wiry gray hair appeared wearing a white coat and a stethoscope around his neck. I had already been taken back for X-rays and was told they would give me medicine for the pain as soon as the doctor okayed it.

"Good news is there aren't any breaks or fractures," the doctor said, pushing his glasses up his nose. "The bad news is that you'll likely have some pain and swelling for a few days, so you'll need to take it easy and ice the area often to reduce the swelling."

A nurse came in and stood beside me as she handed me a pill and a cup of water.

"It's Percocet," she explained quietly as the doctor waited.

I popped it in my mouth and swallowed, thankful to finally have something to help with the pain.

"Do you need a note to excuse you from work?" the doctor asked, pulling out his pen and reaching into his coat pocket.

"No, that's okay. Thank you." I forced a smile but didn't bother to tell him that I would be returning to work tomorrow. If anything, I could ask Bruce to let me work the front registers so I would have minimal walking to do. I needed the hours and wasn't willing to sacrifice them just because my butt hurt.

"Alright, well, you're all set to go. Rest, ice, and pain medication as needed. If it doesn't start to feel better in a few days, be sure to get in with your doctor." He handed Sean the discharge papers.

"Thank you. I will."

I waited until he left before attempting to get off of the bed.

"Here, let me help you," Sean offered, holding his hand out.

"I don't need your help." I swatted him away, refusing to take his hand as I got down and made sure I was steady before attempting to leave. He had been my ride to the hospital, but I had no problem calling someone to come pick me up. "Thank you for bringing me, but your work here is now done."

I went to reach for my phone that was sitting on the table and my eyes widened with disbelief as he grabbed it and shoved it in his pocket before I could.

"What the hell are you doing? Give me my phone." I held my hand out and glared at him as I waited.

"No."

"Are we back on that again?" I muttered, tilting my head to the side.

"Yes. I'm not giving you your phone until I have you safely in my car and take you home. You can fight me all you want, but if you remember correctly, I always win."

"I don't want you to take me home. I want you to leave me alone and go away."

"No can do, Cass."

His eyes locked with mine as he held my gaze, a feeling deep inside running through me at the memories.

"Can you please stop being such an ass about this? Just give me my phone so I can call someone to come pick me up. Like I've said, you've done your part by getting me here, so now you can leave and be on your merry way." I waved my hand to shoo him away.

"Nope. I don't think so. I'm taking you home, one way or another, Cassidy. No matter how much you try to fight me on it."

I tried my best to suppress the growl that started to rise in my throat from my annoyance with him. If he was going to insist on taking care of me, I was going to go out of my way to make it as much of a hassle for him as possible.

Maybe if I showed him just how much of a pain in the ass I could be, he would stop and leave me alone.

"Fine," I said with a heavy sigh. "Let's go."

I tried to lead the way, but his hand on my elbow as he guided me out of the hospital only further irritated me. It wasn't just because of how he was acting—like he had some sort of say in anything regarding me or that he thought he was in control. It was more so because of the stupid tingle I felt down my spine from his touch.

By the time I got situated in his back seat, I was thankful for the strong pain reliever they had given me because sitting on my butt hurt. I tried to lean to the side and take as much pressure off of it as possible, but it wasn't helping.

"Do you want to give me your address, or should I just drive around town asking people if they know where you live?" Sean asked, meeting my eyes in the rearview mirror.

"I have some stops I need to make on the way," I grunted, frustrated with not being able to get comfortable.

"Okay. Where to first?"

His lack of being frustrated about me asking him to take me places really got on my nerves. If anything, he almost seemed *excited* to spend time with me and didn't care that I was asking him to chauffeur me. Not to worry, I would quickly change that and make him regret wanting to do the nice thing.

"Coffee."

"Is Sugarplum Lattes okay?"

I nodded, slowly pushing a breath out through my mouth

as I tried not to cry out in pain. I could feel Sean watching me as he put the car in drive and slowly made his way into traffic.

Once we got to the strip mall where Sugarplum Lattes was located, I unbuckled my seatbelt and reached for the handle.

"What are you doing?" he asked, turning around in the driver's seat with a frown on his face as he looked at me.

"I'm getting out so I can go get coffee," I replied sarcastically. "The drive-through doesn't work unless you actually drive through it, and since you parked, that means I need to go inside."

My head started to feel funny as my body suddenly felt lighter. I knew I was no match for the Percocet they gave me, but it was too late now. It was about to reach its peak, and I would be in for a wild ride.

"Fine. I'll go through the drive-through."

"But I also want some fudge, so I'm going to Sugarplum Sweets too." My voice softened as a rush of euphoria washed over me.

I could see the tightness in his jaw as he clenched it. My evil plan was working and I was getting under his skin just like he had been getting under mine. I hated that I probably wouldn't be awake long enough to actually enjoy it.

"I really don't think it's a good idea for you to be out walking in this." His hands gripped the steering wheel tighter as if he were struggling to stay in control. "The snow is still coming down, and we already know everything is covered in ice. You could slip and fall again, and this time, you might not be so lucky not to break anything."

"I'll be fine. And I'd just like to remind you that *you* were the one who insisted on taking me to run my errands." I twisted my finger in the air playfully.

"Alright, but when you're in more pain later from overdoing it, I don't want to hear it."

"Yeah, well, thankfully, by then, I'll be at home, warm and away from you, so you don't have to worry about that."

Before I could finish my sentence, he had gotten out of the car and slammed his door before coming around to open mine.

<u>Six</u>
Sean

The line in Sugarplum Lattes was almost out the door and I worried about Cassidy standing for so long. She didn't seem to mind as she faced forward and talked to everyone around her but me. It didn't bother me much until I noticed her body start to sway and how unsteady she appeared to be. Not only that, she turned and smiled at me which was a given sign of danger. She *never* smiled at me.

When we reached the counter, her brother Sam was working one of the registers and eyed us cautiously as I guided her forward.

"Hey…" he said, staring at us. "Am I missing something? Are you guys back together?"

"Nope," Cassidy replied, emphasizing the p at the end. "Just came for some java. Some roasted beans. Some of the good stuff. Holly jolly fill you up buttercup goodness."

Sam's brows wrinkled together tightly as he looked from her to me.

"Is she drunk?"

I shook my head and wrapped my arm around her waist as she started to lean against me while sliding down.

"She's on Percocet," I confirmed. "She fell on ice in the

parking lot at Waldon's. I took her to the ER and they confirmed there weren't any breaks or fractures, but gave her the Percocet for the pain."

"Shit." Sam closed his eyes and tossed his head back. "She doesn't handle Percocet well."

"I can see that."

She turned toward me, smiling a smile I never thought I would ever see again, and booped my nose with her finger.

"Hey, Cass," he said, trying to get her attention as he waved at her.

She turned to the side and smiled slowly at him. She reminded me of a sloth with how delayed her movements were.

"Yeah?" she replied, her words slow and drawn out.

"You need to go home and sleep."

She frowned and pouted her lip.

"I want coffee," she insisted. "A mocha cinnamon vanilla latte with extra gingerbread buttery sprinkles."

"That's not even a real drink." He shook his head at the guy working the register beside him as his customer took an interest in what Cassidy was attempting to order. Sam was known for his lattes, and people went crazy every time he came up with a new flavor. This was something I learned quickly in the first few weeks of being back in Sugarplum Falls. The people in Sugarplum Falls were serious about their coffee.

"You need sleep, Cass. Mom and Dad went out of town for

the weekend or I would have you go stay with them since you're in no condition to be on your own until the Percocet is out of your system." Sam rubbed his hand over his face and then looked me in the eye. "Can you take her back to your place until the Percocet wears off? It should only be a few hours, and she'll likely sleep the whole time."

My eyebrows rose dangerously high off my forehead.

"You want me to take her back to *my* house?"

"I know, I'm sorry. I don't have any other options. We're short-handed here today or I would leave and take care of her myself. I hate to ask but if you could help out, I would really appreciate it."

"You do know that once the Percocet wears off and she remembers how much she hates me, there's a good chance she'll try to kill me, right?" I leaned in and lowered my voice so everyone else couldn't hear.

Cassidy leaned against me, her eyes closed as she hummed a song that was too hard to make out. It sounded like a mix between a Christmas song and something from the seventies.

"Would a free latte help?" Sam offered, scrunching his face as he put his hands together and begged.

"It couldn't hurt. Her butt is going to be sore for a while, but I'll need that extra caffeine to get away from her before she tries to kick mine."

Sam chuckled and took my order while I focused on keeping Cassidy upright. She turned into my chest and sniffed the sweater I was wearing, holding it close to her nose.

"You smell like happiness, sunflowers, and wishful thinking," she murmured as I leaned forward to take my drink from Sam while still trying to hold onto her.

Maybe getting a latte was a mistake because I had no idea how I was going to get it to the car while practically carrying Cassidy. I thanked him for the drink and turned just in time to see my parents walk in. My mom's eyes widened with surprise to see me, then narrowed in confusion as she saw Cassidy.

"Hey," I said, already feeling out of breath from trying to carry her and my drink. "What are you guys doing here?"

"We came to grab some lattes before doing some Christmas shopping," my mom answered softly, still staring at Cassidy. "I think the real question is, what are *you guys* doing here."

"*Our* way?" my mom questioned.

I knew how much my parents loved Cassidy and how heartbroken my mother was when she found out we'd broken up. I didn't have the guts to tell her that it was all Declan's fault because I was too heartbroken myself at the time. She didn't seem to know what had happened; she just knew that Cassidy and I had broken up and that Declan and I had a fight that neither of us would talk about.

"I told Sam I would stay with her until the Percocet wore off," I said, pulling myself out of dreadful thoughts about the past.

"Oh. Goodness. Yes. I remember a few years ago when she

had her wisdom teeth pulled. Her mother said she had the hardest time with Cassidy. Apparently, she doesn't react well to it."

"So I'm noticing," I teased, shifting my weight to better hold hers.

"Do you want some help getting that to your car?" my mom asked, nodding to the coffee cup in my hand.

I didn't want to make her lose her place in line, nor did I want to confuse my dad by having her leave.

"Na, but would you mind holding it for a minute?"

She nodded and accepted the cup as I handed it to her. My dad watched and grinned as I carefully bent down and tossed Cassidy over my shoulder, making sure not to touch her ass or the tops of her thighs where she likely hurt the most.

"The world is upside down!" she cheered with a few giggles.

I turned slightly to get her situated as I took the cup from my mom.

"Hello, Mr. Wheeler," Cassidy sang, waving to my dad.

"Hello, dear. It's nice seeing you and Sean together again."

My mom and I exchanged a look, both debating on whether to correct him. There was a good chance he would forget he had said it by the time they got their coffee. I lowered my head and waved at my parents as I carried Cassidy out of the store.

Seven
Cassidy

I woke up to something wet on my face and tried to move away as quickly as possible.

"Max, down," a familiar voice commanded.

My eyes fluttered open as I looked around, not recognizing the room I was in as I spotted Sean in the kitchen. I pushed myself up on the couch, wincing as the pain shot through my butt and thighs as I did.

"Where am I?" I asked, my throat thick and dry.

"My house," Sean replied as he came over and handed me a glass of water. A Doberman Pinscher stood beside him, watching my every move as I lifted the glass to my lips.

"He's friendly," Sean assured me as if somehow reading my mind. "He's just fighting the urge to get up there and lick your face again."

"Was that what that was?" I rubbed the side of my face, not nearly as disgusted as before. I wasn't usually a dog person, but this one was rather cute—but still scary-looking.

"Max likes to show his affection every chance he gets." Sean sat down in a recliner chair across from me and rested his elbows on his knees. "How are you feeling?"

"Sore. I thought for sure the pain would have subsided some by now," I admitted. "Why am I at your house?"

"Your brother asked me to watch over you until the Percocet wore off."

I nodded and pressed the palm of my hand to my head. I knew when the nurse said she was giving me Percocet that it would make me all loopy, but I was in so much pain at the time that I didn't care. I tended to have abnormal reactions to it, which made it last longer in my system than others.

"He did?" I asked, knowing I would dread seeing him and having to deal with his endless barrage of questions. I hadn't even thought about what Sam might think when he saw us together. Out of everyone, my brother knew the heartache I had dealt with after Sean and I broke up and he helped me through it.

"Yup. He even bribed me with a latte."

My head snapped up as my eyes nearly popped out of my head. I remembered being at the counter and trying to order a drink, but everything after that was super fuzzy.

"My brother had to *bribe* you with coffee?"

Sean nodded with a faint smirk on his lips.

"Wow. What a brother."

"Well, there weren't many options. He said your parents are out of town, and he was short-handed, so he couldn't leave work. It was either leave you in my care or take you home and risk you parading down Main Street singing Christmas carols at the top of your lungs."

"That happened one time," I said, pointing a finger at him. "And that wasn't even because of Percocet. That was a few too many Dirty Reindeer Balls at Sugar Faced Bar. I blame Aiden for that."

"Well, either way. It seemed like the safest option was to have you stay here until the Percocet wore off."

"Thankfully, it seems to have already done that, so I can call a cab and get out of your hair. I wouldn't want my brother to have to bribe you with anything else since I was such an inconvenience."

"No one said you were. He was teasing about bribing me with the latte, Cass. I would have done it either way. And I hate to break it to you, but I don't think you're getting a cab in this weather," Sean said, nodding to the TV that was on but muted. He grabbed the remote and turned it up as the local meteorologist pointed to a map showing the expected snowfall Sugarplum Falls was due to get tonight.

"This is a massive storm," she said, shaking her head in disbelief. "We have several reports already of traffic accidents due to black ice and strong winds. The Sheriff's office is asking that everyone stay off the roads until this storm passes. We all know what that means. Stay home, stay warm, and check on your neighbors to make sure they have the supplies they need to get through this one. But if you don't have to be on the roads, don't."

The news report ended and went into a cheery commercial about buying your loved one a brand-new car this holiday season. *I mean, seriously, who has that kind of money to spend on Christmas?* But that wasn't even the biggest problem. This storm was already on top of us, which meant there was no chance of me getting back to my place tonight after all. I sank lower on the couch as dread and disappointment washed over me.

"Are you saying I'm stuck here with you?" I finally asked, allowing myself to look at him. I knew the answer, but it felt better to ask anyway, just in case some miracle dropped out of the universe and presented itself.

"It sure looks that way."

Eight
Sean

"Dinner will be ready in a few minutes," I said, knowing Cassidy was awake because I just saw her reach for her phone on the coffee table.

She hadn't taken the news of being stuck together lightly, but at least she finally listened when I told her to lie down on the couch so she could alleviate some of the pain. I'd given her an ice pack and some more Tylenol for the pain since I didn't have anything stronger, and we didn't have a chance to fill her prescription before the storm hit.

"I'm fine," she called back with the same attitude she had before she fell. I hated to admit it, but I kinda preferred Percocet Cassidy. She was a lot nicer and less of a pain in my ass.

"You're going to eat," I warned, stirring the mashed potatoes to mix in the butter and milk.

"And you're going to make me?"

"If I have to, yes."

"I'd like to see you try."

I wiped my hands on a kitchen towel and then tossed it on the counter before stalking into the living room and standing over her. Thankfully, it was an open-concept room with the living room and kitchen separated by an island, so I'd been able to keep an eye on her while I cooked.

"Why are you so defiant?" I asked, arms folded tightly over my chest.

"Because you're not the boss of me and I don't know why you think you are."

"I'm not trying to be the boss of you, Cassidy. I'm being hospitable and offering you food while you're staying with me. There's a difference."

"Yes, and no one asked you to. I appreciate the offer, but I'm fine."

"Look, I get it. I know you have strong feelings about me, and that's fine. But can we agree to let the past stay in the past for the next twenty-four to forty-eight hours until this storm passes?" I asked with more than a hint of frustration.

"Are you asking for a temporary truce?" she asked, lifting her hand as Max adjusted beside her on the couch. *Traitor.* From the moment he met Cassidy, it had been instant love and he'd abandoned following me around to lay protectively beside her on the couch.

"Yes." However, I wouldn't be opposed to a permanent one either.

"Fine. But only because I don't want to be any more miserable than I already am."

She shook my hand and I fought to ignore the way my body wanted to pull her against me and hold her like I used to.

"Now that that's settled, dinner is ready."

I let go of her hand and walked into the kitchen before I could do something I would regret—like kiss her. I didn't expect her to be comfortable sitting at the kitchen table, so I plated her food and then delivered it to her on the couch. Before she could object about eating there, I lifted the top of the coffee table, turning it into a table for her. I was determined to take care of her the best I could, which meant getting ahead of fights before she could start them.

"Thank you," she said, looking at me from under her thick, dark lashes.

"You're welcome. Would you like something to drink besides water?"

"I'm good, but thank you."

"I have orange soda," I offered, waiting to see if she still lit up about it the way she used to.

"You drink orange soda?" she questioned, holding her fork in the air as this news took her by surprise.

"No." I shook my head and laughed.

"Then why do you have it?"

"Because I know you like it."

"So you've just been storing it at your house, waiting for the day I fall on my ass and you have to come to my rescue?"

"No," I replied with a chuckle. "But that would make quite the romance story, wouldn't it?"

A faint blush flushed her cheeks red before she looked away.

"I had some groceries delivered earlier when we got here. I knew I wouldn't be able to get to the store while you were sleeping, and I didn't want to risk not having stuff you liked before the storm came. I wasn't sure how long you would be here, but I wanted to make sure you had what you might need."

"You didn't have to do that." Her voice was soft and sent a dagger straight into my heart.

"I know. I wanted to." I swallowed the rest of the words in my throat, along with the emotion blooming inside my chest as I headed back into the kitchen to get it for her.

Nine
Cassidy

"I still can't believe you learned to cook like this," I said, blotting my mouth with a napkin as I tried to get the barbeque sauce off. Sean had made pulled pork smothered in a homemade barbeque sauce with mashed potatoes that were to die for. I couldn't remember the last time I had tasted something so good.

"There's a lot about me you don't know."

"I guess time will do that to people," I commented before realizing the weight of my words.

While we had agreed to a temporary truce until the storm passed and I could go home, that didn't mean I wanted to dig up the past. There were a lot of things that had gone unsaid over the years, and now wasn't the time to say them.

"I made brownies for dessert and ordered a carton of vanilla ice cream to go on top," he said, redirecting the conversation for us.

My cheeks flushed as I noticed how many little things he did to make sure I was comfortable in his house on such short notice. The fact that he remembered most of my favorites was impressive. It wasn't like I didn't remember his from back in the day, but guys didn't seem to ever remember those details *while* you were together, let alone twelve years later with no contact during that time.

"Thank you. That sounds delicious." I finished my food and set my fork on my plate before looking down to see how to lower the top of the coffee table so I could get up.

"I got it," Sean said, sweeping in to help me lower it before grabbing my plate and collecting my empty soda can.

"I can help clean up dinner," I offered, attempting to stand.

"I appreciate the offer, but I would like it if you rested instead. The remote for the TV is right there if you want to find a movie or something for us to watch." He nodded to where it was sitting on the end table and then headed into the kitchen to clean up.

I grabbed it and refused to allow myself to feel the butterflies that threatened to overcome me with thoughts of past movie nights with Sean when we were dating. It was our favorite thing to do back then, and we made it a weekly thing. Every Friday night, we would order dinner or pick it up, then cuddle on the couch and watch movies until curfew came around. Back then, we both worked part-time jobs and could afford to go out, but we preferred our nights in together.

I flipped through the channels, not sure what he would want to watch. There weren't a ton of options other than sports channels and a few cooking shows. I kept going until I found a Christmas movie, figuring why not try to get in the holiday spirit. It wasn't that I wasn't excited about it this year; things just felt busier all around, and drawing Sean's name in the Secret Santa exchange really soured my mood. It was hard to want to buy for someone when you held such hostile feelings toward them. While I wanted to hate him and hold on to the anger that had consumed me all those years ago, I was finding it harder to hold a grudge against him for how nice he was being.

"If you don't like anything on TV, I have subscriptions to a few streaming services," he offered from the kitchen as he finished loading the dishwasher. Max laid in the middle of the room, equal distance between Sean and me as if he couldn't decide who to be with.

"You can pick if you'd like," I replied, extending the remote to him as he came in and sat down in the recliner across from me. Max jumped up with him, nearly knocking the chair over with his weight as he struggled to get as close to Sean as possible.

"I'm good with whatever you decide. We can binge Christmas movies if you wa—"

His sentence was cut off as the power went out from the storm raging outside.

"Well. Okay, then. Or not." He chuckled lightly as he got up and used the flashlight on his phone to make his way into the kitchen. Within a few minutes, we were bathed in soft lighting as candles flickered around us.

"That storm is getting worse," I commented as the wind howled and tree branches whipped against the windows.

"Yeah, they said it was supposed to get pretty bad. It's been a while since I've had to deal with weather like this, but it's funny how it all just comes flooding back to me. I found myself in total prep mode earlier when I was placing the grocery order and made sure to get extra batteries and canned goods, just in case."

"Thankfully, it's not usually this bad, and since you live so close to Main Street, they'll likely get the roads cleared fairly quickly. It's usually those who live further on the outskirts of town that get hit the hardest."

"That's good to know. Sorry about the movie. I would offer something else to fill the time, but I haven't unpacked much since I moved in."

"No worries. I'm actually feeling a little tired, so I might call it a night."

"Sounds like a good plan. I'll show you to the bedroom and help you get settled," he offered, coming over to help me up.

"You already have a guest room set up?"

I knew I was stuck staying here with him, but I hadn't stopped to think about what that meant as far as where I would sleep. It seemed a little odd that he would go through the effort of setting up a guestroom when he had only been back a few months.

"Not quite." He pulled his lips into a thin line as if expecting me to be upset.

"Okay. What does that mean?"

"It means there's only one bed, and we're going to have to share it."

Ten

Sean

Have you ever tried to wrangle a rabid raccoon that fell in freezing water, and you're trying to get it to dry land?

Well, that was what it was like trying to get Cassidy into my bed.

Not that I was trying to get her *in my bed*. Nope. I was simply just trying to get her in it so she could close her eyes and get some sleep so she could wake up and choose violence again in the morning. But apparently, she wanted to choose violence now instead.

"It's not that big of a deal," I objected, standing in the doorway with my arms outstretched so she couldn't try to take off running again.

I had carried her down the hallway and insisted that she take my bed, but she refused. There was no way I was going to allow her to sleep on the couch in the living room with all of the full-length glass windows and a large sliding glass door. That room was hard enough to keep warm with the heater on full blast when the power was on, and unfortunately, being a lumberjack hadn't been on my list of priorities when I moved back, so I didn't have any wood for the fireplace.

"I am not sleeping in your bed." She stood in front of me, arms crossed and nostrils flaring.

"You're being ridiculous. It's just a bed."

"No. It's *your* bed."

"And I have some sort of cooties or something?" I questioned with an arched eyebrow.

"Probably. Not to mention that I vowed I would *never* sleep in your bed again after we broke up, and I take that vow seriously."

"Cass, that was over twelve years ago. You need to let it go and move on with your life."

"Ha! You, of all people have no right saying that."

"Yet here I am saying it. It's getting late, and as much as I love this new found combat with you, I would like to get some sleep. I've already told you that I will sleep on the couch and you can have the bed. Take it."

"No."

"Do you just not know any other words besides no?"

"I know plenty. Most of them are considered offensive to most people, so I save them all for when I talk about you." She pursed her lips and narrowed her eyes.

I let my head fall forward as I struggled not to let my frustration overcome me.

"Cassidy. It's negative ten degrees outside. There is at least four inches of snow that has fallen in the last hour. The wind gusts are strong enough that they have downed the power lines, making it impossible to heat the house. I am not going to stand here and fight with you all night about where you're going to sleep."

"If you can sleep on the couch, why can't I?"

"Because I would feel better knowing that you're warm and comfortable in here. Even with ten blankets on, it's going to be freezing in the living room. I don't have wood for the fireplace, so unless I throw a bunch of random shit in there, we don't have that as an option tonight. I would rather be the one to suffer an ungodly cold night tonight than allow you to. I would do anything to make sure you have what you need, Cassidy."

Cassidy's face suddenly fell as she tried to look away before I could see it.

"What? What was that look for?" I asked, stepping closer to her so she couldn't avoid me.

I knew I was risking my life but I didn't care as I lifted her chin with my finger, forcing her eyes up to mine.

"What was that look for, Cassidy?"

"It was nothing."

"Nope. You're not getting out of this one that easy. You've been a hellion on steroids for the past thirty minutes and have damn near tried to kill me at least seven times. Suddenly your mood switches, and I don't get to know why? I don't think so. Tell me."

She rolled her eyes and attempted to break free from my touch, but I held on tighter.

"Now, Cassidy."

She glared at me, her anger returning full force as she reached up and swatted my hand away.

"I told you it's nothing. Just a simple moment of me having a weakness over how kind you were being, but I'm over it."

"Bullshit."

"Don't believe it if you don't want to. I honestly couldn't care less."

"See, the problem is that you do care. I can see it in the way you're avoiding looking at me and how your lower lip keeps trembling." I reached out and brushed my finger against it to drive home the point.

"Do you really want to know why I don't want to sleep in your bed?" she asked, cocking her head to the side.

"Yes."

"Because once upon a time, your bed was my favorite place to be. It was where I felt safe, and I wanted to stay there forever. Then you went and ruined it for us. Sleeping in your bed only reminds me of what we used to have and how you stole that from us with one stupid mistake. So, no, I don't want to sleep in your bed and be tormented by memories of when we used to be happy together because those days are gone, and my heart can't handle the hurt you caused. You being nice to me right now just further deepens the hurt because I don't want to like you again, Sean. I don't want to risk letting you back into my life—even as a friend—knowing the damage you can do."

A stray tear slid down the side of her face as she quickly wiped it away.

My heart felt like it was going to explode in my chest. I wanted to tell her the truth about how none of that had ever happened, but I knew she wouldn't believe me. She didn't back then, and she definitely wouldn't now. She would think I was just saying it to get my way, which was the last thing I wanted.

I shoved a hand through my hair and exhaled sharply.

"Let me grab some extra blankets, and I'll help set up the couch for you."

I walked out of the room before she could say anything.

Eleven
Cassidy

The tension was thick between us as Sean worked on piling a few pillows onto the couch and tucking in a thick blanket. I knew I had hurt him with what I said, even though that wasn't my goal. I didn't want to hurt Sean, but that didn't mean *I* wasn't still hurting from what happened between us. Back then, I convinced myself that I was too young to know what love felt like and that my heartbreak was so hard because I didn't just lose a boyfriend; I lost my best friend. But deep down, I'd always wondered if he really was my first true love.

He finished what he was working on and left the room, leaving Max sitting beside me as we waited for his return. I hated that I was stuck here for the foreseeable future, especially now that we had this giant elephant in the room that neither of us wanted to deal with.

"Here, put these on. You'll stay warmer," Sean said, returning with a pair of sweatpants and a sweatshirt.

"I'm fine. Thank you."

"Cassidy, I'm not in the mood to fight with you anymore tonight. Please just put these on so I can rest knowing you're not freezing your ass off."

I could hear the pain and frustration in his voice, so I took them and tried to smile, but it fell short. I walked past him to the bathroom and changed. It was surprising how soft and warm they were, but the worst part was that the sweatshirt smelled like him.

When I returned, he was putting a blanket down on the recliner.

"What are you doing?" I asked, stopping in my tracks as I watched him.

He looked over his shoulder and then turned his attention back to the chair.

"Making my bed."

"Why? You have an actual bed. You should go sleep in that."

"I don't think so."

"Why not?"

He finally stopped and turned to face me. His features were hard, and there was a furrow between his brows.

"Because, Cassidy, I'm not going to go sleep in my bed while you freeze out here on the couch."

"So you're going to torture yourself by trying to sleep in that thing?" I pointed to the chair that didn't look nearly long enough, even in a reclined position, to fit him.

"Sure am."

"Sean, you're being ridiculous. Just go sleep in your bed. I'll be fine in here. I have plenty of blankets and warm sweats. It's not like I'm camping out in the wilderness."

"No, but this room gets cold quickly. It's the one thing I hate about this house. I'm not leaving you in here to suffer while I'm warm and comfy in my bed. So either you come sleep in my bed with me, or we both camp out in here."

Max laid down on the hardwood floor and whimpered, probably from how cold it was. I knew that he wasn't going anywhere without Sean and that he would be more comfortable in the bedroom. So technically, I wasn't making a decision that benefited Sean; I was thinking about poor Max and his comfort.

"Fine. We'll sleep in your room."

It hurt to say that because the thought of being in his bed again sent a flurry of emotions rushing through me. I didn't want to have to think about the past or have the memories of happier times with him. But he was right. This room was already painfully cold, even with the warmer clothes on. It was stupid to make everyone suffer by sleeping in here just because I was hung up on the past.

"We don't have to. I don't want to make you uncomfortable."

"It's fine," I assured him for a second time. "We'll all sleep in the bedroom."

"In the bed," he added, giving me a stern look.

I rolled my eyes and headed for his bedroom without replying. Max stayed on my heels until we got inside and then cuddled up in the soft bed tucked in the corner of the room. It surprised me that he didn't sleep in the bed with Sean, given how clingy he was. But then again, I couldn't imagine that Sean was the kind of guy who wanted a dog sleeping on top of him—which was likely no doubt what Max would do if given the chance.

"Which side do you want me on?" I asked, waiting before I got in on the wrong side.

"Whichever side you want. It doesn't matter to me."

I looked around and noticed which nightstand had more items on it, and went with the opposite side. I pulled the blanket back and climbed in, already hating how much I loved the softness of his bed. The mattress was thick and immediately pulled me in, making me want to never leave again.

I felt the bed shift slightly as he climbed in beside me. He was right; it was a lot warmer in the bedroom, likely due to there being only one small window hidden behind heavy curtains. I pulled the blanket up tighter around me and closed my eyes as sleep quickly took me.

In the morning, I woke up to Sean painfully close to me as his warm breath tickled my neck. My eyes fluttered open to find his face right next to mine and one hand resting on my hip. Before I could move and try to get away, his eyes opened and locked onto mine.

"I thought I made it clear last night that me sleeping in your bed didn't mean you had any right to touch me or try to cuddle," I said, pulling my head back as far away as possible. The last thing I wanted was for him to think this was okay.

"You did," he replied, his voice still filled with sleepiness.

"Okay, then please explain to me why you're in my face and why your hand is on my hip."

"Technically, *you're* in *my* face. And my hand is on your hip to keep you from kneeing me in the balls again."

My eyebrows pinched together as I stared at him in confusion.

"What in the world are you talking about? You're clearly the one violating the *no-pass* zone we established with the rolled blanket last night. It was there for a reason. To keep you on your side and me on mine."

"Yeah, and as you can tell, that didn't work so well. Not only did you encroach on my space, you brought your barrier along with you. Look over your shoulder, and you'll see what I mean."

I cautiously glanced to the side and gasped in horror as I saw all of the space on the other side of the bed where I was supposed to be sleeping. I propped myself on my elbow and looked over at his side to find him right on the edge of the mattress. If he rolled even half an inch, he would be on the floor.

"Sean!" I exclaimed, smacking him on the shoulder.

"What?" he held his hand up defensively so as not to lose his balance and fall off the bed.

"Why didn't you wake me up and tell me to move back to my side of the bed?"

"You were sleeping well, and I wanted you to get rest."

"So you just slept on that tiny sliver of mattress all night and let me knee you in the balls?"

"No, technically, you didn't start moving this way until around four this morning. I couldn't tell if you were having a bad dream or not, but you rolled over and grabbed me. You were breathing heavily and kept crying, but then when I put my arms around you, you stopped. I don't know what the dream was about, but it seemed to end once you cuddled up next to me."

I covered my face with my hands and groaned.

"Oh my God. That's so embarrassing."

"Why is it embarrassing?"

"Because it is. I mean, who does that in their sleep? Not only did I make you hold me, I nearly pushed you off the bed. Trust me—that's embarrassing."

"It's not a big deal. I got plenty of sleep, and it appears you did too. That was the goal, so it doesn't matter how we got there. Plus, it was a lot warmer with us sharing body heat. But the good news is the power came on sometime this morning, so I can make some coffee and breakfast if you're hungry."

I knew he was just doing all of this to be nice because we were stuck together, but I hated that, deep down, I missed being with him. I missed what could have been if he hadn't messed things up for us when we had a chance.

Twelve

Sean

By the time the storm stopped and the roads were clear enough for Cassidy to go home, it had been three days that she had been stuck with me. I had hoped that it was enough time to get her to lower her walls and hear me out so I could explain what happened twelve years ago, but I had no such luck.

It wasn't just me who missed having her in the house— mainly in my bed. Max hadn't stopped moping around and whining when he'd lay on the couch where they used to cuddle when she was there. My constant companion who used to follow my every move now cared less about where I went and what I did. I couldn't blame him because her absence made me depressed as well.

A whole week had gone by before Cassidy and I worked a shift together. Waldon's had started their extended holiday shopping hours, meaning they opened earlier and stayed open later, so we had a lot of shifts that were opposite each other.

Waldon's had been especially busy today with it being less than two weeks until Christmas and people struggling to get their shopping done. I headed into the break room after Bruce forced me to take a lunch break and was pleasantly surprised to find Cassidy in there having lunch with Rachel.

I grabbed my bag from the fridge and sat at one of the tables across the room from them to give them privacy since Cassidy had her back to me and hadn't seen me come in yet. I pulled a sandwich out and unwrapped the saran wrap before taking a bite.

"I don't know what to get her," Rachel said, tossing a corn chip in her mouth. "When I ask her what she wants, she gives me this long list of things she makes up in her head. Like a robot elephant that blows bubbles and then poops turds when he's done. That doesn't even exist!" She threw her hands up in frustration.

"Five-year-olds can be hard," Cassidy agreed with a laugh. "What about one of those robot dogs we just got in?"

"She already has one. I swear, this kid has *everything*. It's hopeless. I'm going to be the mom who ruins Christmas because I don't know what to get my kid. Even her list to Santa wasn't helpful. It was just more of the stuff she made up."

"Oh, man. That has to be hard."

"It's so difficult this year because she's old enough to decide what she wants on her own, but yet she gives me nothing to work with."

"What about arts and crafts stuff?" Cassidy offered.

"She has a ton."

"Legos?"

"We have enough to make a complete replica of Sugarplum Falls and all of its residents," Rachel said sarcastically.

"Well, shit. I'm running out of ideas." Cassidy crumpled up

the foil her sandwich was wrapped in and tossed it into the trashcan beside them.

"What was your favorite gift when you were a kid?" Rachel asked, leaning back in her chair as she took a swig from her can of soda.

"Hmmm. That's a tough one. I think it was probably a book called *The Christmas Cabin* that my grandmother bought for me. It's this fun story about this big family, and as the children grow up, they get too busy to spend time with their loved ones during the holidays. So their parents buy this old, rundown cabin. They call each child out at a different time throughout the year to help fix up a portion of it. They never tell the other kids what is going on, and since the children are always so busy, they never check in with each other. Then, one day, all of the children get a letter in the mail inviting them to the Christmas Cabin.

When they get there, they find their parents and see all of the work that's been done at the cabin. They realize that each of them helped build a portion of it, and hanging on the wall is a collage of photos that is built like a puzzle. Each picture is of the adult children coming to work on it and the progress they made. There's a lot more that I won't get into, but at the end, they all get stuck at the cabin because of a big storm, and no one cares because they are happy to be together again. It's basically that the Christmas Cabin worked magic and made them remember the importance of family and being together."

"Aww. That's a cute story. I bet Sharon would love it. Do they still sell it?"

"Unfortunately, no. I somehow lost my copy a few years

ago and haven't been able to find one since. I've looked everywhere for a new copy but haven't found anyone that sells it. When my grandmother passed, it broke my heart that I lost her and the gift she had given me."

"I'm so sorry," Rachel said.

"It's okay. Things happen. But I would give anything to have that book again. I used to read it every year right before Christmas and it somehow always made it feel like the holidays were so magical."

"I definitely need some magic on my side this year. I work every day until Frosty Fest, but I can't even take a day off because I promised the kids I would take them to the parade. You and I both know that you can't go just for the parade. It ends up being an entire day thing with shopping and hot chocolate and more sugar than anyone needs in a single day."

"Yup. But that's what makes Frosty Fest so fun. I'm off that day, too, so maybe I'll see you guys there."

I wanted to stay and listen to Cassidy talk, but I knew it wasn't my place to keep eavesdropping on their conversation. I got up from the table and threw the rest of my lunch away, knowing that I had startled them by the sudden movement when Cassidy spun around and looked at me. I gave them a quick wave as I rushed out the door, determined to find the impossible.

Thirteen
Cassidy

"I cooked last week," I complained, rolling my head on my neck as I stood in my parent's kitchen.

"Did you? I can't remember anything this time of year. All of the days start to blend together." My mother shook her head and pushed her glasses back up her nose as she flipped through pages in the cookbook she was looking at.

"I did, and I think this week is supposed to be Sam's week."

"Well, he can't make it tonight so I guess that leaves one of us."

"Fine. I'll cook tonight, but only because you and Dad will be cooking Christmas dinner next weekend, and I want no part of it," I teased. "Besides, I think he does this on purpose. Lies about having to work late just to get out of cooking. It's funny how he rarely misses Sunday dinner on the weeks one of us cooks."

It wasn't that I didn't want to help them cook; it was that I wanted to make tonight easier for my mom by taking the pressure off of her to cook. I was tempted just to give in and order pizza, but I could tell how stressed she was already and didn't want to add to that. Growing up, her parents had traditions that they never deviated from, especially this time of year. That meant that these traditions had also been passed down to my brother and me, so I knew how important they were to her.

We were ten days away from Christmas, and she was supposed to start all of the holiday baking. I knew the recipes by memory, so it surprised me that she had to look them up.

"What are you looking for?" I asked while gathering the stuff from their fridge to make chicken alfredo.

"The recipe for the raisin cookies," she replied, still flipping through the pages.

It was a cookbook that had been put together several decades ago and passed down from generation to generation with the family recipes. It had seen better days and some of the paper had gotten so thin and worn that it had to be laminated and secured in a clear sleeve to keep it from getting further damaged. I had offered at one point to type everything up, but she scoffed and said I couldn't ruin the magic of the book by doing that.

"Aren't those from Dad's side of the family?" I asked, looking over my shoulder as I cut the chicken breast into thin slices.

"Oh my gosh. You're right." She closed the book and tilted her head up in frustration. "He's been asking for them and I didn't even think to look in the other book. I swear, my head would spin off if it weren't attached."

"Is everything okay? You seem more stressed this year than normal."

"Yeah," she replied with a wave of her hand. "I'm fine. I'm

just getting older, and when that happens, things feel like they get harder and harder. I used to be able to bake dozens of cookies over a few days and not miss a beat. Now just the thought of baking them makes me tired."

"I can come over this weekend and help if you want?" I offered.

"Isn't this weekend Frosty Fest?"

"It is, but only on Saturday. I'm off on Sunday, so I can hang out, and we can spend the day baking. I can see if Sam is free, too. We can make a family baking day out of it."

"I would really like that."

My mom smiled softly and gently squeezed my shoulder as she passed by to put the cookbook away.

Thankfully, dinner was relatively quick and easy to make. We sat down at the table to eat, even though it felt weird not having my brother there. It wasn't unusual for one of us to have to miss Sunday dinner at my parents' this time of year, but I felt like I hadn't seen him in weeks.

"So, have you finished your shopping?" My dad asked as he twirled noodles around his fork.

"More or less. I have a few more gifts to get for you guys and Sam. I also have to do the stupid Secret Santa gift exchange at work and haven't bought for that person yet." I clenched my teeth. Just the thought of trying to figure out something to get Sean really irritated me. I wanted to be mad at him and hate him the way I used to, but he'd really worn me down the three days I had to stay with him. Now I felt even more conflicted about what to get him because I didn't want to give the wrong impression that I liked him, yet I didn't want to be a cold-hearted bitch and get him a shitty gift because that wasn't fair after everything he'd done for me recently.

"Oh yeah? Who did you draw?" Mom asked.

They knew I had stayed with Sean for a few days when the storm hit, and they hadn't stopped talking about second chances and how great of friends we used to be. It had been stressing me out because the last thing I needed was for them to be hopeful that Sean and I would ever get back together.

"Sean," I answered quietly, avoiding direct eye contact.

The sound of her fork hitting her plate caught my attention as I looked up and found her with a delighted smile on her face. Great. Just great.

Fourteen
Sean

"Are you sure they're up here?" I asked, moving boxes around in the attic at my parents' house. Friday was my first day off in a while, and I'd told my mom I would come over to find the rest of the Christmas decorations she was looking for and help her finish decorating.

"They should be. Your dad said he put everything away last year when we took down the decorations. I mean, I guess it's *possible* that he put them somewhere else by mistake…"

I could hear the worry in my mom's voice as she stood below me, holding the ladder in place.

"Then I'm sure they're here," I tried to assure her.

"Do you need some help?"

My blood turned to ice as I heard my brother's voice.

"No. We're good," I replied sternly, not bothering to look at him.

"Hi, honey," my mom said sweetly. "Sean is just looking for the box that has all of the lights for the house, and then we can start decorating. Did you have any trouble getting checked in at the hotel?"

"None at all. Everything went smoothly. Stephanie and the girls are there now. The girls were still sleeping, so I told Stephanie I would catch a cab and come early so she could have the car to head over when they were ready."

I stopped what I was doing and turned to stare at my twin brother.

He hadn't changed much over the years, but then again, neither had I. His short hair that barely touched the nape of his neck was a stark contrast to how long he used to keep it. At least now it was out of his face.

"You got married?" I asked gruffly.

He nodded, shoving his hands in his pockets as he rubbed his lips together.

"Five years ago. We have twin girls that just turned four last month."

I looked from him to my mom, wondering why she never said anything. She'd been a grandma for four years, and yet I had no clue.

"Why didn't you tell me?" I asked her as I climbed down the ladder.

She shrugged as a blush turned her cheeks red with embarrassment.

"You made it very clear that you wanted nothing to do with your brother. Every time I tried to bring him up, you'd shut me out. I gave up. I realized many years ago that until you two settled whatever this fight was between you, I would have to have very different and separate relationships with my boys."

My jaw clenched tighter as I stood in front of my brother, taking him in.

"Did you cheat on her too?" I asked, loving the way he flinched at my words.

"No." He lowered his head in shame. "I'm sorry for what I did when we were young and stupid, Sean. But I've changed a lot since then. I'm not that kind of person anymore. It would be great if we could move past it because I would really love for you to be part of my family again."

"*You* cheated on your girlfriend in high school, then lied and said it was *me*," I growled, poking him in the chest with my finger as my mom let out a gasp. "To this day, Cassidy still hates me because of what *you* did. How am I supposed to just forgive you when you ruined the greatest thing that ever happened to me?"

"Look, I've said I'm sorry. I don't know what more you want from me, Sean. It's not like I can go back to the past and fix things now."

"You're right. You should have fixed them then. Instead, you acted like a coward. You let me take the fall for your betrayal. Cassidy has looked at me like I'm a monster ever since, and it's all because of you, you selfish piece of—"

"Okay!" my mother snapped, putting her hands up and stepping between us. "That is enough out of both of you. I don't care about what happened in the past. I care about right now and giving your father the Christmas he deserves. He spent his life bending over backward to take care of this family, and I'll be damned if we don't do the same. So figure out how to put your differences aside and be the men I raised you to be."

She looked at each of us, silently putting us in our place.

"Yes, ma'am," I replied, refusing to meet my brother's eye as he studied me. "I'll work on finding the rest of the lights if you want to go check on Dad."

"Thank you. I appreciate it. Declan can stay out here and help you."

"Mo—"

"I will *not* hear any excuses about why you two cannot pull your heads out of your asses and figure this out," she warned, pointing her finger at us as she headed back inside the house.

The door closed, leaving a deafening silence as my brother and I stared at each other.

"I don't care what Mom says," I told him firmly. "Stay out of my way."

I went back up the ladder and tried my hardest to forget he was still standing there.

A few minutes later, I heard him rummaging through boxes on the other side of the garage and was thankful that he wasn't going to force any interaction between us. We were both here for our parents and to focus on giving my dad a Christmas he would hopefully remember. Everything else could wait.

Fifteen
Cassidy

It had been a long day at work, so an evening in cozy pajamas with a pepperoni pizza and a bottle of wine was just what the doctor ordered. Okay, so I was now technically referring to myself as *doctor*, but it made me feel better. Plus, it was a Friday night, and I had the next two days off of work.

There was nothing on TV, so I played on my phone, browsing social media until I got bored. I had already wrapped the majority of the gifts I'd purchased and stacked them neatly under the tree in my living room. I still had a few people left to buy for, but I planned to see what I could find at Frosty Fest tomorrow.

Almost everyone I knew in Sugarplum Falls waited to finish their holiday shopping until after Frosty Fest. It was a huge thing in town, and people came from all over to attend it. We'd also gotten vendors who came from neighboring towns, which made it easier to find those unique gifts people were always looking for.

But while Frosty Fest could solve a lot of other problems, it couldn't solve my current dilemma about what to get for Sean. I'd been racking my brain for weeks with not a single idea of what would make a good Secret Santa gift. It wasn't just that I didn't want to be an asshole and get him a terrible gift; it was that these gifts would be opened at the annual Waldon's holiday party that was *two* days before Christmas. So not only would he get to see what I got him, but all of our coworkers would see as well.

I opened a new browser on my phone and typed: *what to get someone you hate for Christmas.*

I stifled a giggle as I took a sip of wine and read the list of the top ten gift ideas.

1. *A donation in their name; that way, they actually get nothing*
2. *Self-help books*
3. *Something messy for their children if they have them*
4. *A super loud chew toy for their dog if they have one*
5. *A candle in a scent you know they don't like, or your favorite scent so they have to think of you whenever they smell it*
6. *A calendar of animals pooping*
7. *A t-shirt printed with your face on it*
8. *A candle shaped into a hand with the middle finger lifted*
9. *A bag of their least favorite snack or a gift card to a restaurant they hate*
10. *A poem about all the ways they annoy you and why you hate them*

By the last item, I had laughed so hard that I nearly spit my wine out and choked. None of these were things I would ever consider for Sean, except maybe getting him a vanilla-scented candle that would make him think of me. But that was definitely hitting below the belt and had the potential to backfire by making him think that I liked him again.

I closed the browser and opened one of my online shopping apps, hoping something would jump out at me. There was less than a week until Christmas, and I couldn't afford to show up to the party empty-handed. There had to be a gift out there somewhere that said *I don't quite like you, but I don't hate you either*, and I was determined to find it.

Sixteen

Sean

My body was tense and rigid as I sat at the table, unsure how to act around my brother's wife and two little girls as they joined us for dinner. I found the missing decorations my mom had been looking for and helped her finish putting them up while Declan worked with my dad to restock the wood for the fireplace.

Stephanie and the girls arrived a few hours ago, but I'd purposely made myself busy to avoid having to interact with anyone. When my mother said my brother would be coming to town for Christmas, she could have mentioned that he had a family he was bringing with him. I knew that she had wanted to keep her distance from the fight we had going on between us, but this was important information, and I hated being blindsided by it.

"Can you pass the gravy?" my mother asked after handing the bowl of mashed potatoes to Stephanie. I reached for it at the same time as my brother, pulling my hand away before he could touch it.

"Daddy, can you open this for me?" Jocelyn asked, handing me her bottle of apple juice.

"Umm," I said, frowning as I looked at it. I didn't mind opening it for her, but I didn't want her to continue thinking I was her father.

"That's Uncle Sean," my mother replied, not bothering to ask if I minded that they called me that. Sure, I was technically their uncle, but that didn't mean I was ready to wear the title. "And yes, he can open it for you, Jocelyn."

I pushed out a quick breath and then gently took the bottle from her little hands. Once it was opened, I gave it back, watching to make sure she didn't spill it before setting it on the table beside her food.

"Why does he look like daddy then?" Carly asked, pointing at me.

"Because he's your daddy's twin brother. They are identical twins, which means they look a lot alike. Just like you girls," Stephanie explained, brushing a strand of brown hair out of her daughter's face.

"How are we supposed to know who is daddy then?" Jocelyn questioned, her curiosity valid.

"Well…" Stephanie started, looking at my brother with pinched brows.

"You just call me daddy, and I'll answer," my brother replied before taking a bite of his food.

"Or, you can look at their eyes," my mother added. "Your daddy has a small mole right by his left eye, and Uncle Sean does not."

Both girls turned to look at their dad's face before turning to study mine. I could only imagine how confusing it was for them to find out that their dad had a twin brother and seeing me for the first time. Stephanie seemed to know about me, but I had no idea what all Declan had told her about why we weren't close anymore or if he had told her the real reason for our falling out twelve years ago.

"So," my mother said, changing the subject. "Your father and I are heading over early to get seats for the parade tomorrow. Sean, you're welcome to ride with us if you'd like to. I'm sure you remember how busy it used to get when you still lived here, but it's even bigger now, and parking is hard to find."

"Yeah. Sure. Sounds great." I took a bite and tried to swallow but nearly choked when she continued.

"Declan, you guys can meet us here and then follow us over. That way, we can all sit together for the parade."

I closed my eyes and tried to hold back the groan that desperately wanted to come out. I knew my brother would likely want to take the girls to the parade so they could see the reindeer and Santa, but I didn't expect us to be doing *everything* as a family. It was hard enough pretending to like him when no one was around, but it was pure torture to put on a fake act for his daughters.

Once everyone finished with dinner, I volunteered to do the dishes so I could avoid having to be around Declan. I was filling the sink with hot water when I noticed someone standing beside me at the sink.

"I know that you need space from everyone, but would you mind if I helped you with dishes? I could really use a break right now," Stephanie said with a heavy sigh.

"Umm. Sure."

I didn't know her well and didn't want to be rude by telling her no.

"Is everything okay?" I asked, my innate desire to fix everything rising to the surface from the sound of distress I recognized in her voice.

"Yeah. It's just hard this time of year, know what I mean?" She pushed the sleeves of her sweater up and looked at me as we stood side by side at the sink. "Sorry," she said, shaking her head. "Of course you don't know what I mean. You didn't even know we existed until a few hours ago and now some strange woman who's married to your brother wants to babble on about the stress of the holidays with two small children."

She laughed nervously and reached for the stack of plates sitting on the counter.

"How about I wash and you dry?" I offered, noticing how out of place she looked and not wanting to cause her any more stress.

"Okay. I can put things away, too, if you let me know where they go."

I nodded and took the plates from her as she walked to the other side of me and turned the water on. I scrubbed the first plate with soapy water and then handed it to her, both of us working in silence for a minute as we got into a groove.

"Is there anything specific that's stressing you out about the holidays with the girls?" I asked, not sure why I was taking the time to find out. It wasn't like I was planning to have a relationship with my brother, so there wouldn't be any relationships with his wife or children either. But I was by nature a problem solver and couldn't seem to help myself.

"They're getting older and they understand more now," she started, glancing up at me as she took the next plate to rinse it before setting it on the rack with the rest she was going to dry. "I want to create the magic for them, but I don't know how. I grew up in a house that didn't celebrate the holidays, so this is all new to me. When Declan and I got pregnant, he told me about all of the fun traditions you guys had growing up, and that's what I want for our girls. But I don't know how to do it. I know that sounds weird, but none of this feels natural to me."

"What kind of traditions are you trying to start?"

"Well, I wanted to do the stuff he told me about, like opening one gift the night before Christmas and giving everyone a new set of pajamas so we can cuddle together on Christmas Eve and watch movies. But then I hear about this elf thing, and I feel like the girls would like that, but I don't even know where to start with it. Do you know how hard it is to find a little elf?"

"I do, actually," I replied with a grin. "I work at Waldon's, which is basically a giant store with everything you could ever need. I can't tell you how quickly we sold out of the elf-on-a-shelf dolls we had there and how many extra orders we had come in that sold out right away. They're so popular, we can't keep them on the shelves. We even have people from neighboring towns that drive all the way over to grab one."

"Great," she said with another heavy sigh. "I thought I might be too late for it this year. I keep trying so hard not to ruin Christmas, but it feels like I'm doing everything wrong."

I let the plate I was washing sink to the bottom of the sink as I dried my hands on a towel and turned to face her.

"You're not ruining Christmas for them, Stephanie. Even if you got an elf, they likely don't even know what it is or what they're supposed to do. Maybe you save that for next year, when they start school and their friends talk nonstop about it. Then you guys can plan ahead and get one early so theirs can show up and cause trouble with everyone else's."

"Thank you. That's very sweet of you. And you're right; they wouldn't know any more about it right now than we do. Maybe it's better to wait until they're a little older. I just want to make sure they have fun and that they stay excited for Christmas."

"I get that," I said as I resumed washing dishes while she worked on drying the stack of plates she had. "But there's a lot of fun, *easy* stuff you guys can do to keep them excited. Like the Frosty Fest—all of the kids love that. From what I've heard, there will be a pen where the kids can feed the reindeer. Plus, they'll have a chance to see Santa and Mrs. Claus and get pictures taken."

"I think they're super excited about the reindeer." Stephanie laughed, sounding less stressed. "Your mom promised to take them to a few stores, and I guess she's getting some sugar cookie sets that you can decorate?"

"Probably from Sugarplum Sweets. I heard Andi, the owner, was doing toddler sugar cookie decorating classes, but they might be over now. I know I saw some of the decorating kits in the shop, though, so I'm sure my mom already grabbed some before they sold out."

"Yeah, I believe she said she wanted to do pizza tomorrow night for dinner, and then she wanted to get everyone together to decorate the cookies on Sunday. You'll be there, right?"

Just then, Jocelyn came into the kitchen, tugging on

Stephanie's shirt as she tried to get her attention.

"I think I work that day," I lied, hoping she didn't hear it in my voice.

"You're not going to decorate cookies with us?" Jocelyn asked, pouting.

"You're not supposed to be listening to adult's conversations," Stephanie told her softly as she bent down to be on her daughter's level. "You know that."

"I'm sorry." Jocelyn's little eyes started to water as she lowered her head. "I just really want Uncle Sean to help me with the cookies."

Stephanie looked up at me with an apologetic smile, but it wasn't her fault that her daughter shot a dagger straight into my heart.

I knelt down, getting on Jocelyn's level with Stephanie.

"If it would make you happy, I'll come help decorate cookies," I told her, giving her a genuine smile.

She released her grip on her mother and launched herself into my arms, nearly knocking me off balance as she wrapped her little arms around my neck.

The way my heart felt like it was going to explode from the unconditional love my niece was giving me was too much. I looked up just in time to see my brother in the doorway, watching us.

Seventeen
Cassidy

"I need another gingerbread latte," I told my brother as I stood in line at the pop-up booth for Sugarplum Lattes for the third time in an hour. Frosty Fest was in full force with people everywhere and lines at all of my favorite booths.

"No," he replied, giving me a concerned look. "You're going to be wired for days."

"Come on, Sam," I groaned, letting my head fall in frustration. "I need the caffeine boost to help me think."

"Think about what?"

"Finding the *perfect gift* for a *not-so-perfect* person," I said grumpily.

I was at my wit's end trying to come up with something for Sean. I'd gone from store to store to store, coming up empty-handed every time. I'd even checked out all of the booths set up for Frosty Fest and still couldn't find anything worthy of a Secret Santa gift for someone you sorta hate. I did, however, find plenty of stuff for myself that I didn't need.

"You still shopping for Sean?" he asked as he made a latte for someone else.

"Yes. Now can I please have my latte so I can go on my way and be miserable somewhere else?"

"Nope. But I will make you a chocolate raspberry hot chocolate," he offered, raising an eyebrow as if he didn't know this was my weakness.

"Fine. But when I crash out in Sugar Faced Bar, I'm blaming you."

"Well, I'll give Aiden a heads up to watch for you and deny you service when you get there."

"You wouldn't!" I gasped, clutching my chest as he worked on my drink.

"Oh, I would. Drunk, stressed-out Cassidy is just as bad as high as a kite on Percocet Cassidy. No one needs that right now," he teased.

"You know, I'm not sure I like you very much," I teased back. "Maybe I'll go exchange your gifts and buy myself a nice bottle of wine or some truffles from Sugarplum Sweets."

"An ax," he blurted out randomly while putting a lid on the to-go cup he handed me.

"What? Are you threatening me? I was just kidding about taking your gifts back, Sam."

"For cutting wood. Sean mentioned the other day that he hadn't had a chance to gather wood before the storm hit. I asked if he wanted me to come over and help, but he said no because he needed to get a new ax. The one he had broke."

"You want me to buy the guy I hate, and who I'm pretty sure doesn't like me much either, an ax?"

"No, Cassidy. I want you to buy the guy you once loved

and were best friends with a gift that he could use. Something helpful and thoughtful instead of some rude and insulting gift because you can't get over the past and the hurt he caused twelve years ago. You're not seventeen anymore. It's time to move on and let all of that go. It's not healthy to hold on to grudges like that. Like Grandpa used to say, every ounce of anger you hold onto is an ounce of happiness you miss out on instead."

I inhaled deeply, allowing the air to move through my lungs before slowly letting it out.

He was right. It was time to move on and forget the past. The thing was that it wasn't just the past that I was worried about. It was about how I currently felt about him and the realization that maybe I didn't hate him as much as I once thought.

I thanked my brother for the drink—which he refused to accept payment for—and went to finish my shopping. While I liked his idea, I wasn't sure that *Sean* and *ax* belonged in the same sentence.

Eighteen
Sean

"Okay, where to next?" I asked as I looked down at both of my nieces holding my hands. I had no idea how I had gotten roped into this, but I also found that I didn't mind one bit. While my relationship with my brother was strained, there was a love deep inside of me for these two little girls and I wasn't about to let my issues with him taint my new relationship with them.

"Can we go feed the reindeer again?" Carly asked, looking up at me with blue eyes that mirrored mine.

"I think the reindeer are too full to eat anything else right now," my mom said from behind us.

I glanced over my shoulder to find her with her phone pointed at us as she took a picture.

"I'm tired of not having the memories I want to cherish," she explained with a stern look, not that I was going to object. If anything, I would be sure to find somewhere festive where the girls and I could sit so she could get a better picture. Then, I would bug her until she printed a copy for me to hang proudly in my house.

"We could go get some lunch," Stephanie suggested as she and Declan walked beside my parents.

It felt weird being at Frosty Fest in general, but even more so being there with my entire family. We had plenty of people stop us to say hi and meet Declan's girls, but it was almost as if the past twelve years had passed in the blink of an eye.

"That's not a bad idea," Declan agreed. "They turn into little monsters when they get hungry."

The girls started giggling as he reached forward and tickled their sides.

"I'll get Joceyln, and you get Carly. Whoever gets there last is a rotten egg," he said, nodding to me. I had no idea what he was talking about, but then he reached down and pulled Jocelyn onto his shoulders. She laughed even harder as he held onto her hands to keep her steady.

"Oh, we're racing now?" I said, surprised by the joy that was pushing a smile across my face. "You ready to beat them?" I asked Carly, looking down at her as I realized I was unsure how to get her on my shoulders without hurting her.

"Here, let me help you," Stephanie offered, clearly seeing the dilemma I was facing. I bent down, waiting as she carefully put Carly on my shoulders. Following Declan's lead, I held onto her hands and made sure she was steady.

"On your mark. Get set. Go!" my mother said, squealing as I almost bumped into her to get around my brother.

It was too packed in the mall to be doing this, but the way the girls were laughing kept me from caring. We zoomed in between tables, neither of us sure where to go.

"Over there," Carly instructed, pointing to a sign with a chicken wearing a hat.

"You got it!" I held her tightly as I weaved around a few tables and then jumped into the line before Declan could.

"Sucker," I teased, glancing over my shoulder as he came up behind us, out of breath like I was.

"You cheated."

"How so?"

"You knew where the chicken place was."

"Not really. I don't come to the mall often, and this was never here when we were growing up. I just went where Carly told me to go, so you'll have to be mad at her for us beating you guys."

Declan bent down and helped Jocelyn off of his shoulders before pulling Carly down from mine. The girls stood in front of us as they talked about what they wanted for lunch. I wasn't sure what *yummy sauce* was, but they knew for sure that they wanted it.

"Thanks for being nice to my girls," Declan said quietly with a soft smile. "I know you don't care for me much, but I'm really grateful that you're not letting my girls see it."

I felt my jaw tense as I thought about how to respond to him. It had been over twelve years since our falling out, but that didn't erase seventeen years of him being my best friend.

"They deserve to get to know their uncle," I replied, keeping my focus ahead of me instead of looking at him. "Even if I missed the first four years of their lives."

"It wasn't like you would have answered your phone to talk to me if I would have called to tell you about them."

"Probably not. But I still would have liked to know."

"I'm sorry."

I nodded, letting a slow, deep breath leave my lungs.

"For everything, Sean. I'm sorry for all of the hurt I've caused and for ruining what you had with Cassidy. I was stupid back then, and I should have done the right thing. There's not a day that goes by that I don't regret what I did. If I could go back in time and make it right, I would."

The line started moving, giving me the space I needed to process what he said while he ordered food for his family.

Nineteen
Cassidy

"Sorry I'm late, but I come bearing coffee," Sam said as he walked into my parents' kitchen, which was covered in flour and baking utensils.

"If you don't have a gingerbread latte, I'm going to—"

"Relax," my brother replied with a chuckle. "I have your gingerbread latte, and mom's peppermint mocha, and dad's black coffee. Trust me, I know what everyone likes by now."

"Well, some of us have been up baking since the butt crack of dawn and need an afternoon pick me up," I said, narrowing my eyes as I accepted the drink he handed me. "Thank you."

"Yeah, and some of us have been up since three this morning making lattes to keep the crazy town of Sugarplum Falls running," he countered. "Some of us need the afternoon pick me up more than others."

"Has it been that busy?" my dad asked, taking a sip of his coffee.

"Yeah. I don't know why, but people are way more stressed about Christmas this year than usual. We've had lines out the door since we opened, and the drive-thru line has blocked traffic on Main Street. Piper is closing today, but I imagine she'll stay open late to get through the line."

"Wow. I didn't know people were so stressed right now," my mom said with a cinnamon stick poking out of her bun.

"Mom, you have cinnamon in your hair," I commented, pointing to it.

She reached up and felt around until she found the cinnamon stick.

"Oh, my goodness. I thought that was a pen." She looked around the messy kitchen that had cooling racks scattered about with stacks of cookies on them. "I wonder what I did with the pen."

My dad leaned over the pot that was boiling on the stove, using the tongs to pull something out.

"Found it," he said, holding up the dripping wet pen.

"Oh my God!" I burst into laughter, making everyone else laugh with the snort that came out with it. "Mom!"

"What? I'm sorry, but things have been busy, and I've been distracted. It's not my fault. This is why I said we should have just gotten everything from Sugarplum Sweets and saved everyone the trouble this year."

"Yeah, but I like our family tradition," I said softly.

Sure, the day was long, and my feet would be killing me by the time I sat down, but I wouldn't trade this for anything in the world. Baking as a family were some of my fondest memories growing up, and spending time in my grandparent's kitchen as we learned from them.

"Mine too," Sam replied, hanging his coat on the back of a chair. "Even if I'm always late and miss most of it. I still enjoy being here and doing this as a family."

"Well, I don't know about you guys, but once I finish this latte, I'm bringing out the *real* afternoon pick me up," my mom said, nearly downing her latte in one big gulp.

Sam and I exchanged a look with each other before staring at our mom in disbelief.

She set her empty cup down and then went to the fridge.

"Eggnog, anyone?"

Sam and I both groaned, knowing that my mom's eggnog always messed people up. She didn't bother to measure when she made it, which meant it was usually stronger than anything Aiden served at Sugar Faced Bar.

"I'll order the pizza," Sam said as I pulled off my apron and hung it on the wall.

"I'll start cleaning up."

We all knew that once the eggnog was out, that was the end of family baking because no one wanted to bake while they were buzzed—and we would all end up that way if we drank it. On nights like this, it was common for Sam and I to stay the night, so we didn't have to worry about driving home. While I still had my old bedroom to sleep in, Sam would crash on the couch, which he claimed was more comfortable than his old bed that my parents got rid of when they converted his room into a craft room for my mom.

An hour later, I was resting on the couch with my feet up, enjoying the warm fire as I finished my second cup of eggnog. The pizza was supposed to arrive any minute, but I could already feel the warm fuzzies creeping into my head.

I grabbed my phone and opened the text messages. It had been over twelve years since I had called or texted Sean, but I never had it in me to delete his phone number. I chewed my nails as I debated sending him a text message, hoping he hadn't changed his phone number.

He had been overly nice to me when he took care of me after I fell, and it wouldn't hurt me to say thank you for it. It wasn't like I was forgiving him or professing my love for him—just a simple *thank you*.

I scrolled through the names in my phone until I found the one that said *Fucker Face*. I clicked on it and started writing my message.

Me: Dear Sean. I am sorry.

I squinted at my phone to try to read the words, but everything was blurry, and it looked like it was spinning around me. I pressed send and then started another message.

Me: You are not an ass, but you have one.

Me: A nice one.

Me: I wasn't looking.

I looked up as my mother stood in front of me, offering me a refill of eggnog. I smiled and took it from her, wondering why it was sloshing around so much. I took a big sip to bring the level down before it spilled.

Me: But maybe I should.

I was about to text more until Sam sat beside me and yanked my phone away from me.

"Hey! What are you doing? Give that back," I demanded, holding my hand out.

He grinned as he read through the messages.

"Who is *Fucker Face*?"

"None of your business," I snapped, lunging for the phone as the liquid in my glass rose dangerously close to spilling over again. I took another drink, wondering why my mother kept refilling it if it was already full. Then I found her sitting on the other couch with my dad, drinking her glass of eggnog. I frowned at the one in my hand and wondered if it had somehow been reproducing on its own and making more when I wasn't looking. Maybe it was one of those cheeky little elf dolls. Those things gave me the creeps.

"Is this Sean?" he asked, a wicked grin spreading tightly across his face as my phone dinged with a new text alert.

"Give it to me!" I set the glass down the best I could on the table beside me and lunged for my phone.

"What's going on?" my dad asked, watching us. It wasn't unusual for us to wrestle when we were younger, but those days were long past us. Or so I thought.

"Nothing," I grunted. "Sam is being an ass and won't give back my phone."

"Language," my mom scolded, followed by a hiccup.

"I'm twenty-nine, mom. I say much worse than that when you're not around."

"Doesn't surprise me one bit," she answered, lifting her glass but pausing to take a drink as she hiccupped again.

"It seems our little Cassidy is texting Sean," Sam said with a mocking tone.

"Oh! How lovely!" my mom exclaimed, attempting to clap her hands until my dad intervened and took her drink away. He never partook when we had eggnog, which was probably best since we all needed an adult to supervise us. "I'm so happy our little Sean Cassidy is back!"

"Your what?" I asked, stopping to try to get her face into focus. Man, that eggnog was strong this time.

"Our little Sean Cassidy. That's what we used to call you two back in the day when you were dating."

"I don't even know who that is," I said with a shake of my head and a shrug.

"You know, Sean Cassidy?" she pressed, tilting her head to the side.

"Not ringing a bell."

"*The Hardy Boys Mysteries*?"

I shook my head again, wondering if Sam knew who she was talking about.

"Well, he might have been a bit before your time. But back in the day, he was a real looker, and all the girls loved his voice."

"Sounds fabulous," I said with a hint of sarcasm. "But no, *we* are not Sean Cassidy. There is a Sean, and there is a Cassidy, but we are not together."

"Might want to check your phone before you start denying anything," Sam teased, tossing it back to me as he got up to use the restroom.

I looked down at the screen, and my eyes widened.

Fucker Face: Feel free to touch it if it makes you feel better.

Twenty
Sean

"Okay, what did I miss?" I asked as I joined my family at my parent's large dining room table. We had already decorated cookies, watched movies, and ate pizza. Now we were having a game night, and the girls wanted to play Uno, even though they had no idea how to play.

"You're a fish!" Carly exclaimed, giggling behind her hand as she held her cards in front of her.

"That was the last game, sweetie," Stephanie said, laughing at how much fun her daughters were having.

"Oh yeah!" Carly pressed the palm of her hand to her forehead in true dramatic fashion.

I had been distracted since I first got a text message from Cassidy, but my mind had been wandering ever since she mentioned my ass. I couldn't tell if she was drunk or if someone else had taken her phone and was texting me for her. Just when I was expecting the text messages to stop, another one came in. I grabbed my phone and checked it while the girls bickered over what game to play next since they were now bored with Uno.

Cassidy: Who said I want to touch it?

My lips curled up into a smile as I debated on how to respond.

Me: No one. But you are the one who brought up my ass to begin with.

Cassidy: All I'm hearing is that you're an ass, which I strongly agree with.

Me: Just a few minutes ago, YOU were saying how I wasn't an ass. So which is it?

Me: Did you mean to apologize, or are you on Percocet again?

Cassidy: Wouldn't you like to know?

I raised my eyebrows and nodded my head, even though she couldn't see me. I would like to know so I could make sure she was safe and not home by herself in an altered state. If she was willing to text me, she was probably drunk on Percocet.

Me: I would.

Cassidy: Why are you so obsessed with me?

Me: I'm not. But I do worry about your general well-being and about making sure you're taken care of.

Cassidy: Like you used to take care of me behind the bleachers at school?

A whoosh of air escaped my lips as my mind started racing with memories of said bleachers.

"Hey, sorry, but I gotta go," I said, excusing myself quickly. "I'll call you later with my schedule this week so we can talk about Christmas Eve."

I waved at everyone, ignoring the confused looks from my mom and Declan as I rushed to say goodbye to Stephanie and the girls before jetting out of the house. My dad was outside, fixing a broken light on the house as I breezed past him.

"Bye, Dad!"

"See ya, Sean."

I climbed into my car and pulled my phone out to see if she had sent anything else.

Cassidy: Do you remember that? Lifting the skirt on my cheerleader uniform so you could finger me until I came?

"Fuck," I groaned, my dick immediately hardening.

Me: I remember very clearly. You were always so wet for me.

Me: Are you wet for me right now?

I knew it was pushing every line I shouldn't cross, but I didn't care. Twelve years or twelve seconds didn't make a difference when it came to Cassidy. I wanted her just as much now as I did back then.

Cassidy: Maybe.

Me: You're making my dick hard just thinking about it.

I fastened my seatbelt and peeled out of the driveway, desperate to get as far away from my parent's house as possible before my dick exploded. I was a grown man, but that didn't mean that I had any self-control when it came to Cassidy. I drove a few miles until I was out of town and pulled over on the side of the road.

Cassidy: I miss your dick. It was always so hard and big.

Me: It misses you too.

Cassidy: I always had the hardest time taking all of it in my mouth. It used to hit the back of my throat, and I had to use my hands for the rest that didn't fit.

Me: You always took it so well, though. Such a pretty mouth that sucked me off so good.

My balls were aching as I tried to restrain myself from jacking off. I wanted to come so badly, but I wanted to do it with Cassidy there—not that it was even an option.

Cassidy: I'm going to send you something. Hold on.

I frowned, wondering what she was talking about until a picture message popped up. I gripped my phone hard in one hand while biting down on my knuckles on the other. She was fucking killing me with the picture of her pussy barely covered by a sheer black thong.

Me: You're killing me over here, Cass.

Cassidy: Then do something about it.

Me: What do you suggest?

Cassidy: Jack off and send me a picture when you're done.

I quickly undid my belt and zipper, pulling my cock out in record time. I turned on the camera on my phone and pressed record as I started stroking my cock. I gripped the shaft hard, trying to keep from coming right away, but it was too hard when all I could think about was Cassidy's pussy.

I pumped quicker, feeling the build-up as I imagined her lips wrapped around me as she took me to the back of her throat like she used to. I wanted to bury my face in her pussy and lick up her arousal more than I wanted my own release. Just the thought of her touching herself right now was more than I could take. I kept stroking, my body tensing as I came hard, ropes of cum shooting all over my hand and thigh.

I pressed the button to stop recording and grabbed some napkins to clean up. Not knowing how she would take it, I went ahead and sent the short video to Cassidy.

Twenty-One
Cassidy

I woke up with a headache and drool on the side of my mouth as I reached around to find my phone that was obnoxiously loud with the alarm I'd set going off. I had to work today, and I knew yesterday that I needed to set at least seven alarms to make sure I got there on time, thanks to Mom's eggnog.

When I unlocked the screen to silence the alarm, I noticed a new text message from Sean. My memories of last night quickly flooded my brain, and panic consumed me as I rushed to read through the messages I'd sent, hoping it had been a dream—or more so, a nightmare. To be nice to Sean while under the influence of eggnog wasn't something that should be allowed to happen. Sam should have confiscated my phone or something once he figured out who I was talking to. Talk about *not* being a good brother.

My eyes widened in horror as I covered a hand over my mouth while reading them. Not only had I been nice to him, I had sent him a naughty picture of my legs spread and my sheer black panties.

When I got to the end of the thread, there was a video from Sean. I had asked him to jack off and send me a picture, but this wasn't a picture. It was a video, and I didn't have to guess what it was about.

My finger trembled slightly as I pressed the button to play it, making sure the volume was down. The last thing I needed was for one of my family members to think I was up watching porn at seven in the morning in my childhood bedroom.

The screen was dark but clear enough that I could see he was inside his car as he gripped his dick and stroked it. A heat started building between my thighs as I watched him jack off and come on his hand. I quickly exited out of the video and tucked my phone underneath my pillow as if that would protect me from what I'd just seen.

I got up and started gathering my stuff so I could go home and get ready for work. It was going to be beyond busy for the next few days until Christmas, which meant I would need extra caffeine to keep me going.

****

By the time I got to work, I was twenty minutes late. I had called Bruce to let him know ahead of time, and thankfully, he wasn't upset. I had to forfeit my stop at Sugarplum Lattes and settled on a few energy drinks I found in my fridge when packing my lunch for the day. I didn't love them, but they got the job done.

I clocked in and looked at the schedule, frowning when I found that I was working in the back today. We had two trucks that had been unloaded this morning, and now my job was to spend the day organizing the inventory so the night crew could restock the shelves for tomorrow.

I pulled a hair tie out of my pocket and put my hair into a high ponytail, ready to get this over with. There was a lot to work through, so I planned to start with the toys since I knew they would be a top priority. If, for some reason,

I wasn't able to get everything put away before tonight, at least they could get those restocked before we opened tomorrow. It would save whoever was working in the toy department the hassle of constantly coming to the back to see if something was in stock or not.

By the time I made it back to the pallets of toys, I looked up and frowned again when I saw Sean.

"What are you doing back here?" I asked, my mood already sour.

"Working," he replied casually with a glance at me before returning his focus to the pallet he was unloading.

"Why? I'm on the schedule for this today. Not you."

"Bruce asked me to get started since you were running late."

"Yeah, and now I'm here so you can go."

"I don't think so."

"Why not?" I demanded with my hand planted firmly on my hip.

"Because I already got started and am in a groove. Plus, with both of us working back here, it'll get done faster."

"Yeah, but you can go help someone who is actually happy to see you today," I said, practically sneering.

Okay, so it wasn't his fault that I was in such a bad mood. I was embarrassed about what happened last night and not ready to face him yet. Add in the way he kept looking at me with that stupid shit-eating grin, and I wanted to chuck a rock at his head just to get it off.

"Well, that's unfortunate because *I* was really looking forward to seeing and working with *you* today."

My cheeks flushed with embarrassment as I picked up on his tone. It was obvious that I wasn't going to catch a break today and that we would be stuck together after all.

I rolled my eyes and ignored him as I walked past the pallet he was working on and started working on another. We worked in silence for a while, somehow managing to stay out of each other's way. It was probably because there were so many pallets of toys and different aisles they all went on, so it allowed us to not have to be in each other's space.

A few hours later, Bruce came back to check on how things were going and complimented us on how efficiently we were working together. I smiled, though deep down, I wished he knew how much restraint it took to keep me from hitting Sean with the broomstick ponies I had just finished unloading.

We got down to the final pallet of toys, and I stood back while Sean cut the plastic covering off it.

"I've got this one if you want to go start on the food," I offered, hoping he would take me up on it.

"Food is already done," he said, pulling the plastic down. "Tom and Gabe worked on it this morning. All that is left after this is housewares."

"Oh. Okay. Well, then, you can go to housewares."

"That's okay. I like to finish what I start."

A shiver snaked up my spine as I focused on his words and wondered if he was talking about what had happened last night. I tried my best to ignore it as I reached for a stack of boxes and bumped into him in the process.

"We're going to have to figure out a way to work around each other if you're going to insist on staying in my space," I said curtly, avoiding his eyes as he towered over me.

"Maybe you're the one in *my* space."

I swallowed hard as he took a step forward, forcing me to take a step back to avoid our bodies touching.

"I'm not. I was assigned to work back here. You weren't."

"Well, it seems fate had other plans."

I moved further back, a gasp escaping my lips as my back hit the metal rack behind me.

"I wouldn't call it fate. I would call it you being obsessed with torturing me and forcing yourself into my space today," I said, looking away as he stood inches away from me.

He licked his lips as he rested one hand above my head and spread his feet to lock me into place. Unless I injured him, there was nowhere to go.

"Do you want to know what real torture is, Cassidy?" he asked, my name sounding like sin rolling off of his tongue. He turned his head to the side and studied me, his gaze hot as it penetrated me.

"Being stuck with you?" I offered, smirking when I felt his body tense around me.

"Nope. Real torture is getting that picture of you in those fucking panties last night and not being able to touch you.

Having to remember how tight you were and not being able to fuck you."

I tried to swallow, but my throat was suddenly dry as a burning heat blazed between my thighs.

"Sounds like a *you* problem." My voice was barely above a whisper, but he heard me.

"Not really. I *took care of* the problem. Remember?"

My skin prickled as a rush of heat washed over it.

"No," I lied, desperately trying to look anywhere but in the deep blue eyes that were watching me.

He leaned closer and slowly brought his hand up to cup the side of my face. His touch was feather soft until he pinched my chin between his fingers and turned my head, forcing my eyes to meet his.

"Did you watch the video?"

"No," I lied again, this time sounding breathless. Goosebumps covered my skin except the places his fingers touched, which left a trail of heat behind.

"Are you sure about that?"

I nodded, not making any effort to break free from his touch this time.

"Then why are you blushing?" He pulled his lower lip between his teeth as he waited for my answer.

"I'm not. It's hot back here."

"Liar."

Shit.

"You don't have to be embarrassed about watching it, Cass. I sent it to you because I wanted you to watch it. I wanted you to see what you did to me. How hard you made me just thinking about the ways I wanted to touch you."

Another wave of heat poured over me as the ache between my legs started to build.

"You forget how well I know you. How well I know your body."

"I seriously doubt that. It's been over twelve years. Don't flatter yourself."

"I'm not. But I would be willing to bet money right now that you're wet for me."

I rubbed my lips together, forcing myself not to answer.

"Are you, Cass? Are you wet for me?"

This was getting dangerously close to me crossing the line and giving in to stupid desire. I needed to stop this now before it got out of control and I did something I would end up regretting. Sean was the enemy, not some old fling I could hump because I was horny.

"Nope. Not even a little. I'm dryer than the Sahara desert."

"Hmmm. Then I guess I have work to do."

"I don't think so, Satan."

"Satan?" His lips spread across his lips in a grin as he nodded. "I'm not usually into that level of role-playing, but I could give it a try. If I'm Satan, does that mean you expect me to punish you?"

"In your dreams." I was running out of witty comebacks—hell, I was running out of words in general. They didn't have to be witty; they just needed to be enough to get me out of this situation. My mind knew what was best for us, but my body clearly had other ideas as it leaned into his touch, and my legs begging to spread for him. *Ugh, stupid body.*

"Well, actually, my dreams are pretty good. Usually they involve us doing all sorts of depraved things to each other and fucking for hours at a time—you know, to make up for lost time."

"Something is seriously wrong with you."

"You're just filled with compliments today, aren't you?" he asked with a glimmer in his eye. He was enjoying this way too much. I didn't have to reach down to see if all of this was arousing him as said arousal poked my leg through his jeans as he pressed himself closer to me.

"Trust me, compliments are the last thing I want to give you." I shoved against his chest, pushing him off of me.

He moved easily, not fighting it at all as he stepped away and gave me space.

"You know what I think, Cass? I don't think you hate me as much as you try to convince yourself you do. I think that you hate *yourself* for still being in love with me."

The air rushed out of me as I processed his words. I narrowed my eyes and pointed a finger, stabbing him directly in the chest.

"You're so full of yourself," I said, shaking my head. "I am *not* still in love with you."

"Am I?" He moved quickly, invading my space again. "Then explain this."

Before I could say anything, his mouth crashed down over mine in a frenzied kiss.

Twenty-Two
Sean

Cassidy's hands tangled in my hair, pulling gently as she deepened the kiss. I lowered my hands and lifted her to my hips, pressing her against the metal rack again. Thankfully, they were all firmly attached to the wall so I didn't have to worry about it crashing down on us.

She whimpered softly as I squeezed her ass, loving how full it felt in my hands. Cassidy had changed a lot over the years, but the thing I'd always loved about her was her butt. Back then, I was a young, horny teenager who didn't appreciate it the way I should have. But I was ready to make up for that now.

"Sean," she moaned as she broke the kiss, her head falling to the side and allowing me access to kiss along her neck.

"Yeah, baby," I said, too consumed with touching her to realize what I'd just called her. She started to slip so I adjusted how I was holding her and pressed her harder against the rack, not failing to notice how our bodies lined up perfectly in this position for her to feel my erection through my jeans. I hadn't had this many hard-ons in who knew how long, but now it seemed like I was constantly sporting one anytime Cassidy was around.

I rubbed myself against her, knowing it was driving her as crazy as it was me by how she pulled harder on my hair and moaned.

"I need you to fuck me," she panted.

"Right here?"

"Bathroom."

I nodded, trying to think clearly. It was as if all of the blood in my body had left my head and was now centered around a different one. Of course she didn't want me to fuck her right here, in the middle of the warehouse, where any of our coworkers could walk in on us.

"I'm going to put you down," I said, slowly lowering her from my body.

She sucked in a shaky breath and once she was on her feet, grabbed my hand and tugged me toward the back of the warehouse where the employee bathrooms were. There were two, both unisex and single occupancy.

I looked around to make sure no one was close by or could see us before I followed her inside and locked the door.

"Are you sure—" I started to ask but was cut off as Cassidy leaped into my arms, wrapping her legs around my waist and locking her hands behind my neck. Her lips were soft as they pressed against mine.

"Cassidy," I warned, breaking the kiss for a split second before she covered my mouth with hers again.

I grabbed her ass, squeezing it tightly as I walked over to the counter and sat her on it. She reached down and grabbed the bottom of her shirt, tossing it over my head as I stared at the black lace bra she was wearing.

"We don't have much time," she said, her tone a warning.

"Are you sure you want to do this?"

"Yes. I'm horny, and we've already slept together before. Isn't there some sort of like hall pass or something where exes can fuck for no reason other than they need someone to get them off?"

"I'm not sure," I replied with a chuckle. "But I thought you hated me?"

"I do. But I also hate being horny. And you have a cock that keeps promising me a good time so I can continue to hate you while you fuck me senseless."

"I don't know if this is the best idea, Cass," I said softly, not wanting to hurt her. But at the same time, I didn't want to go through with this, and then it be something that she regretted.

"I'm not asking you to be my boyfriend or to promise me forever. I'm just asking you to fuck me and maybe make me come. It can be like a friends-with-benefits situation."

"I thought we weren't friends?"

"We're not. But that doesn't mean we can't be fuck buddies. Now, if you don't stop with your million questions, we're going to run out of time to do this."

"Fine," I said, rolling my eyes. "Maybe I can fuck some of that attitude out of you."

"Well, we won't know unless you try, will we?"

I leaned forward and slid my finger down in between her breasts, forcing the clasp that was keeping her bra closed to pop open.

"Sean!" she hissed, reaching for the fabric to cover herself.

"Nope. I'm in control now. You want me to fuck this hate you have for me out of you, it'll be my pleasure. But I say when and how."

Before she could object, I leaned forward and pulled one of her hardened nipples into my mouth, sucking hard the way I knew she liked.

She cried out and arched her back, giving me more access. I flicked the other one with my thumb as I continued sucking, knowing we didn't have the amount of time I needed to do everything I wanted to do to her.

I pulled back and released her nipple with a loud popping noise as she stared at me with flushed cheeks.

"Lift your butt," I commanded, nodding for her to do so.

She lifted herself up while I hooked my fingers into the top of her leggings and pulled them down, groaning when I noticed she was wearing another thong. Those were my weakness.

I gently pushed her back so she was resting on her hands as I lowered myself between her legs. Her thighs parted, inviting me in as I gripped them and held them open while my tongue trailed slowly over her slit.

She moaned softly, her body relaxing against my touch as I parted her with my tongue and slid it inside. My dick hardened even more at the taste of her, begging for a release. I fucked her with it for a few minutes before moving on to suck her clit.

I could feel her body tighten as she got closer and loved that I still remembered all of the things that used to turn her on.

"Shit," she moaned as her fingers dug into my scalp while her pussy spasmed against my face. I pulled back once she was done and smiled, satisfied with how easily I was able to bring her pleasure.

"That was incredible," she said breathlessly as she hopped off of the counter. "But now for the even better part."

She stood in front of me, leaning forward as she rested her chest against the counter and spread her legs. I reached into my wallet and pulled out a condom before undoing my pants and putting it on.

I could see her pussy still wet with arousal as I lined myself up at her entrance. I pushed in slowly, gripping her hips as I watched her eyes flutter closed in the mirror and her lips part. I wanted to take my time savoring her body and fucking her until we were both spent, but we only had a matter of minutes before someone would come looking for us.

"How do you want it?" I asked, my voice gruff.

"Fast and hard," she answered. "Just like the old days."

A shiver shot through me at the memories as I pulled out and slammed back inside of her. She cried out, hands gripping the counter to keep herself steady as I did it over and over. I could feel her tighten around me as I held on tighter and started fucking her the way she needed to be fucked.

Her head tilted back as her back arched, her tits still on full display in the mirror. They bounced wildly with every thrust, making it hard for me not to come right away.

"Fuck," I growled, closing my eyes and gripping her harder as I came.

Twenty-Three
Cassidy

My body was tingling as my mind raced to process what had just happened.

Did I just have sex with Sean in the bathroom at Waldon's?

Yes.

Was it utterly and amazingly fantastic?

Yes.

Did I regret it?

Surprisingly, no.

I didn't have time to try to process why that initial wave of regret didn't come because we were too busy trying to put our clothes on right before we got busted together in the bathroom.

"I'll go out first," he said, his voice soft as a whisper.

I nodded and checked my appearance in the mirror to make sure it didn't *look* like I had just been thoroughly fucked.

He slowly opened the door and stepped outside, leaving it open a crack. I reached for the handle and went to open it when he yanked it shut, startling me.

"Hey, Gabe," Sean said a little too loudly. "How's it going."

"Good." I could hear the uncertainty and confusion in his voice as he answered. "Just working."

"Yeah. Same here. Busy, busy, busy."

"Okay…"

I pressed my ear to the door, trying to hear better.

"Um, are you going in there, or can I use the restroom?" Gabe asked.

"Oh. No. I'm um… I'm done. But you can't use this one."

I pressed the palm of my hand to my forehead and cringed. He was going to find out what happened between me and Sean unless Sean could come up with a believable lie on the spot.

"Why not?"

"It's… out of order."

"Are you sure? I thought the other one was. I've been using this one for the past few days."

"Yeah. I need to let Bruce know, but this one is all clogged up. And it stinks. You don't want to go in there."

"Oh. Alright. I guess I'll use the one by the breakroom. Thanks."

I covered my mouth to keep from laughing and waited for Sean to open the door.

"The coast is clear," he said, opening the door for me to come out.

Before I could ask what that was about, I looked up to find

Rachel heading in our direction with a knowing smirk on her face.

I was still standing in the doorway as Sean attempted to scoot out of the way, but as her grin spread wider, we both knew we'd been caught.

"Hello," she said, practically singing her words. "What's going on back here?"

"Nothing," I lied, feeling the heat burn my skin as my face flushed.

Sean shoved a hand through his hair and looked the other way.

"I was sent to come find Sean," Rachel said, still grinning as she looked between us. "You have some cute little customers up front asking for you."

I furrowed my brow and looked at him.

"Carly and Jocelyn," she added as he seemed equally confused.

"Ahh," he replied, grinning as he nodded. "Thank you. I'll head up there now."

I stepped out of the bathroom and let the door shut behind me as we waited for Sean to be gone.

"Oh. My. God," Rachel squealed, pulling me to the side so it would look like we were working on something instead of messing around on the clock. "Did you and Sean just *ahem* in the bathroom?"

I chewed my lip as I debated on how to answer her. It wasn't like she didn't already know, so it was just a matter of whether I wanted to come clean and have someone to talk to about this or continue to play stupid and lie to her.

"Maybe," I answered, still fidgeting.

"What do you mean, *maybe*? I mean, I get that it had to be a quickie, but was he so fast he didn't even stick it in all the way, or was it so bad that you're not sure if it counts as sex?"

"Rachel!" I shrieked, covering my mouth as I giggled. "Stop it!"

"What? You're the one who said maybe. I'm just trying to figure out what it means."

"It means that, yes, we just hooked up in the bathroom at work."

Goosebumps covered my skin as I remembered the way his body had felt against mine and how good he had fucked me.

"Okay, now we're getting somewhere," she said, pulling out a handful of cheese and cracker sets that we kept selling out of up front. "So, what does this mean? Are you guys back together again?"

I shook my head, grabbing a stack and walking alongside her as we headed back into the store.

"No," I hissed. "We are definitely not getting back together. It was just a quick hookup between two people who once dated. That's all."

"Like a friends-with-benefits situation?"

"No, because we would have to be friends for that to happen. I don't know what to call it. An enemies to fuckers situation? Is that a thing?"

"I don't think so. Plus, don't you both have to hate each other in order for it to be enemies?"

"Trust me, I'm pretty sure Sean hates me as much as I hate him."

"I seriously doubt that. Have you seen the way he looks at you? Do you remember how he stepped in to take care of you when you fell?"

"Yeah, but he was just being nice because he felt obligated."

"Says who?"

I shrugged, not sure how to answer that question.

"Me?"

"Well, I would venture to say you're wrong. You might not see it, but everyone else does."

"See what?" I asked as we walked into the store and headed toward the display where the boxes needed to go.

"That he's madly in love with you. He always has been, Cassidy."

I looked up to find his gaze on mine as he stood in front of two little girls who were bouncing excitedly in front of him. His mother looked up, wondering what had caught his eye and gave me a warm smile and waved. I waved back and then returned my focus to the display.

I didn't have time for emotions right now, especially the kind that made me feel all warm and fuzzy over a guy I once wanted to stab like a voodoo doll.

Twenty-Four

Sean

"Uncle Sean, can you come over for dinner tonight? Nana said she's making pasgetti," Carly said as she tugged on my hand.

"Spaghetti," my mom corrected with a smile. "And yes, dear, you're more than welcome to join us. I'm sending Declan and Stephanie out on a date night tonight and watching the girls overnight while their parents finish their holiday shopping."

"Thank you ladies for the invite, but unfortunately, I have some shopping of my own to finish."

Carly and Jocelyn pouted, breaking my heart.

"I thought you were done?" my mom asked as we walked behind the girls while they headed toward the toy department.

"I was, but then I had a few new people that I needed to buy for at the last minute." I nodded to the girls, and my mom smiled, giving my arm a quick squeeze.

Things had been busy since the day I met them, and I hadn't had a chance to shop for them. I also felt bad not getting anything for Stephanie and my brother, even if things weren't 100% better between us yet. He had apologized, and I appreciated it, but I had a hard time letting go of the past because of how strained things still were with Cassidy because of it. I couldn't help but wonder if things between us would be different if she knew the truth about what happened all those years ago. Not that I hadn't tried to tell her a million times, but I also knew it wasn't *me* she needed to hear it from.

"If you have any ideas of what I can get *them*, I would greatly appreciate it," I said, making sure my mom understood exactly who I was talking about.

She nodded and walked down the aisle, touching certain boxes. When I failed to pick up on what she was saying, she rolled her eyes and pulled the girls to the side.

"Did you tell Uncle Sean about those baby dolls you saw on the TV? The ones that cry real tears and can eat real baby food?"

Their eyes lit up as they both spun around and started talking a mile a minute. While they were facing me, my mom caught my eye and pointed to the box sitting on the shelf beside us, too high up for the girls to really see.

I nodded, making a mental note to get the dolls for the girls. Just then, Cassidy came around the corner and headed our way. She stopped in her tracks, panic written on her face as she spotted me and my mom.

"Hey, Cassidy," I said, locking her in place as my mom turned to see her.

"Hi," she replied, her voice unnaturally high. "Mrs. Weaver, so nice to see you."

"You too, dear." My mother smiled warmly at her as she

stood behind Carly and Jocelyn, resting a hand on each of their shoulders. "I'm not sure that you've met my granddaughters. This is Jocelyn, and this is Carly. They're Declan's twin girls."

"Twins. Wow." Cassidy's eyes were big as she studied the girls with a soft smile. "Nice to meet both of you."

"Nice to meet you too," Jocelyn said with a little wave.

"Do you want to come have pasgetti with us?" Carly asked, tilting her head to the side and batting her eyes.

Oh man, Declan was going to have his hands full with that one.

"Umm," Cassidy hesitated, looking up from Carly to me and my mom. "I'm sorry, but I have to work. Thank you for the invite, though."

"Okay," Carly said, pouting again.

"I should get back to it," Cassidy said, giving us a weird little curtsy bow and then immediately blushing. "It was great seeing everyone. Have a Merry Christmas."

"You too, dear." My mom turned her head to hide the grin that was spreading across her face.

"Hey, Cass?" I said, stepping to the side to block her for a moment. "Can you do me a favor and take these up to the front to hold for a *customer*?" I grabbed two of the baby doll boxes from the shelf and looked at my mom, who nodded with approval.

"Sure. What name do you want me to put them under?"

"F. Face is fine. I'll come take care of it in a few when I go on my lunch break."

"F. Face?" she asked, the name she had so *lovingly* been calling me not registering.

I leaned in and whispered in her ear, *"fucker face."*

I stepped back and grinned at the color covering her cheeks as she took the boxes and walked away.

Twenty-Five
Cassidy

"I didn't know Declan had kids," I said as Sean came up to the front to pay for his stuff.

"I didn't either. Not until a few days ago."

He handed me his credit card after I entered his employee discount and gave him the total.

"How did you not know?"

"I haven't talked to him in twelve years." He shrugged as if this was a totally normal thing to do.

I held his receipt in between us as I pulled my brows in, confused.

"Why not?"

"It's a long story that I don't feel like getting into right now," he replied, his tone a little short.

It wasn't like I didn't know what had happened between *us* twelve years ago, but I never heard anything about something happening between them. I always just thought that they both moved away and went to college. No one ever said anything about there being a feud between them.

"Okay," I said, sighing heavily as I handed him the bags.

He attempted to smile, but it fell flat as he turned and walked away. We were both supposed to be taking our lunch break, but suddenly, I wasn't hungry anymore.

I sat in the breakroom, playing on my phone, when I saw Sean come in. It wasn't like I expected him to sit with me and talk to me about what happened *just* because we had sex not that long ago. But I couldn't help the feeling that gnawed at me that I needed to know what had happened between him and his brother all those years ago. They had always been close, best friends even, so for them to stop talking entirely must have meant that something terrible had happened between them.

He sat at one of the empty tables in the corner and started eating his lunch.

I didn't want to make things awkward between us, but it felt inevitable now. Maybe I was wrong for thinking that we could hook up and then go back to how things were before. The problem wasn't that Sean had done anything wrong. It was that I felt my guard slipping, and I was afraid of what would happen if I let him in again.

"Hello, sorry to interrupt your break," Melissa said, stepping into the breakroom. She was the HR manager at Waldon's and was always cheery and pleasant. "I just wanted to remind everyone of the holiday party tomorrow night at Sugarplum Suites. As you all might remember, the discounted rooms we had secured there sold out very quickly, however, I just got word that someone needed to cancel theirs. So, if anyone wa—"

"I'll take it," I said quickly, raising my hand like a kid in the classroom.

Sean looked up and arched an eyebrow at me.

I had no idea why I just volunteered to take the room, especially since I was attending the party by myself and wasn't planning on drinking, so there was no need to stay there. But for some reason, I just wanted to.

"Well, that was quick," she said with a laugh. "I'll let them know you'll be taking the room. You can check in anytime after 3:00." She waved goodbye to everyone and made her way out of the breakroom while I sat there, wondering why I just did that.

A few other employees finished their lunch and left, leaving Sean and me alone in the breakroom.

"Are you taking a date?" he asked, catching me by surprise.

"No." I shook my head, lowering my phone to the table to give him my attention.

He nodded and took a bite of his sandwich, the muscle in his jaw prominent as he ate.

"Are you?" I questioned, though I didn't know if I wanted to know the answer to that, given we'd just hooked up. But then again, maybe this was something we should have talked about *before* we had sex. It just went to show how clearly I had been thinking before it happened.

"No."

I rubbed my lips and bobbed my head, unsure of how to keep the conversation going between us.

"I don't want things to be weird between us," I blurted out, hating the anxiety in my voice.

"They won't be."

"How can you say that? They already are."

He pushed the last of his sandwich into his mouth and leaned back in his chair as he studied me.

"Things aren't awkward between us, Cass. It's just been a long day, and having *you* bring up my brother just shifted my mood. That's all."

"But why?" I leaned forward, desperate for him to tell me what was going on.

"It just did. I don't feel like talking about it."

"But, Sean, that's not fair. Something serious happened between you guys, and I don't deserve to know what it was?"

"No."

His answer was sharp and quick as his eyes blazed with emotion that I couldn't quite read.

"Really? That's it? Just a *no,* and that's the end of it?"

"Yeah, Cassidy. That's the end of it."

"Why are you being so difficult? It's not like I'm going to go around town spreading gossip about something that happened between you guys years ago. I'm not that person. I just want to know for my own reasons."

"Because it wouldn't matter if I told you what happened."

"Why not? I'm clearly sitting here telling you I want to know." I held my hands helplessly in front of me.

"Because you didn't believe me back then, so why would you believe me now?"

He got up, threw his trash away, and walked out the door.

Twenty-Six
Cassidy

I had the day off, so I got to the hotel early to check-in. It was still fifteen minutes before I could check in, so I sat in the lobby and scrolled through my phone with my suitcase beside me. I didn't need much since I was only staying the night, but I had been able to fit Sean's gift in it, which made it easier not to have to lug a ton of stuff around with me. I'd also added a bottle of wine and a few packs of fudge from Sugarplum Sweets so I could drown my sorrows after the party while soaking in a garden tub.

"Cassidy?"

I looked up after hearing my voice and felt my heart jump in my chest. At first, I thought it was Sean standing in front of me, but I immediately recognized the differences. It also helped that I knew Declan was in town.

"Hey, Declan."

"How's it going?"

"Good," I said, putting my phone down beside me. "How are you?"

"I'm doing good as well. I'm in town for the holidays with my family." He shoved his hands into his pockets and rocked back on his heels as if he was nervous to be talking to me.

"I met your little girls yesterday at Waldon's," I said with a smile. "They were there with your mom."

"They told me. I heard Carly invited you to dinner as well," he replied with a chuckle.

"Yes. I feel bad for breaking her little heart. She looked so sad when I told her no."

"Yeah, she does that. I told my wife, Stephanie, that she gets it from her."

"She most certainly does not," a beautiful woman with long brunette hair down to her butt said as she walked up beside him and locked her arm in his.

"Cassidy, this is my wife, Stephanie. Stephanie, this is Cassidy. We grew up together."

"Nice to meet you," I said, standing up to shake her hand.

"You as well."

"What are you guys doing here?" I asked, immediately hating how rude that sounded. I scrunched my face and shook my head. "I'm sorry. That sounded so rude."

"Not at all," Stephanie replied with a laugh. "We're actually staying here. We were supposed to be going to his parent's house for dinner, but they seem to have kidnapped our children and have given us another date night since ours was tied up in running errands last night."

"Ahh. I see. Well, enjoy your night. I won't keep you guys."

"Not to sound rude either, but what are you doing here?" Declan asked, eyeing my suitcase.

"My work is having their annual holiday party here tonight, and for some strange reason, I decided to take one of the rooms when another employee canceled their reservation. It's silly because I have my own place and can't really afford to be doing this. But here I am." I lifted my hands and shrugged.

"Sometimes fate intervenes and gives us what we don't know we need," Stephanie said. "Maybe this is its way of telling you to slow down and focus on you for a bit. This time of year can get super busy. Do you have kids, too?"

"No." I shook my head quickly. "I'm not even in a relationship."

I swallowed hard as I felt her sympathetic gaze. *Why was I telling them this? They didn't need to know my personal details when they were just being friendly, to begin with.*

"I mean, not that I would mind one, but then again, maybe not. They're a lot of work, and I'm always so busy. It's just not my thing right now." I lowered my hands to keep from talking with them and clasped them in front of me.

"It sounds like you just haven't found the right one," Stephanie said as her words started to fade and her features shifted. "Wait. You said your name is Cassidy?"

I nodded, unsure of where this was going and why she suddenly seemed angry.

She released her arm from her husband's and turned to face him.

"*This* is Cassidy?"

"Yes," he said quietly, looking down to avoid her death glare.

"Umm, I'm sorry, but I can assure you that whatever you might have heard about me is not true. Especially anything about me and Declan. People sometimes get stuff mixed up, but I actually used to date his brother, Sea—"

"You tell her right now," Stephanie said, with her hand planted firmly on her hip.

"I don't think this is the time or place," Declan said quietly, practically talking through his teeth to avoid letting me hear him.

Stephanie turned and looked at me with a smile forced onto her face.

"My husband has something he needs to tell you."

"Okay?" I tried to keep my foot still as it started bouncing up and down nervously on the tile floor beneath me.

Declan took a deep breath in and slowly let it out, looking from his wife to me.

"It was never Sean that cheated on you, Cassidy. It was me."

My eyes bulged, nearly popping out of my head.

"I'm sorry—what?"

"The rumor that went around in high school about someone seeing Sean with another girl—it wasn't him. It was me. I was the one who was cheating on my girlfriend, but I lied and said it was him."

A rush of air blew through my pursed lips as I stared at him.

"Are you kidding me?"

He shook his head and pressed his lips into a thin line as his wife stood beside him with her arms crossed over her chest.

"Why didn't you say something when it happened?"

"Because I was embarrassed that I got caught. I was an immature asshole who didn't know how to own up to my mistakes."

"So you let your brother take the fall for you?"

He nodded.

I could feel my blood pressure rising as anger radiated through me.

"You ruined my relationship with Sean," I nearly shouted, lowering my voice when a few onlookers took interest. "Twelve years, Declan. That's how long I have hated your brother for something *you* did."

"I'm so sorry, Cassidy. I wish I could go back in time and fix everything, but I can't. I messed up so much with one stupid lie, and I deserve everything I've gotten as a result of it. But I am sorry. Trust me, he hasn't spoken to me in twelve years, either. He stopped talking to me the day the rumor started. But I thought for sure you and Sean would be able to talk things out. That you would believe him when he told you it wasn't him."

"Yeah, well, you were wrong about that. I believed the rumor, and because of that, you ruined one of the best things that ever happened to me."

I didn't bother to hear what he had to say as I grabbed my stuff and stormed off.

Twenty-Seven
Sean

The ballroom was already filled with people by the time I got there. Thankfully, Waldon's didn't force us to have a stuffy holiday party with a plated dinner and dress code. Everyone could wear what they wanted, sit where they wanted, and help themselves to the buffet and cash bar.

I found a seat at one of the tables in the back of the room and looked around, trying to see if Cassidy was already there. A few coworkers said hi as they passed by, but I hadn't been there long enough to really make any friends outside of work.

Melissa was up at the front of the room, guiding everyone on where to put their Secret Santa gifts and handing out two drink tickets to those coming in. Cassidy walked in wearing a sparkly black dress that dipped low into her cleavage and had a slit up her thigh. Her black heels made her long legs look even longer, and all I could think about was how good they would feel wrapped around my neck.

I shifted in my seat, trying to force my thoughts elsewhere so I didn't have to excuse myself to deal with the situation building down south.

She set her gift under the tree at the front of the room and then said hi to a few people as she made her way around the room. She glanced at me, and I could tell she wanted to look away, so I held her gaze, making sure she felt the heat from it.

Thankfully for me, the majority of the tables were already filled, leaving mine open for her to join me. She grabbed a glass of wine and came over, seeming unsure of where to sit.

I pulled my arm off the back of the chair next to me and nodded to it. She rubbed her lips together as if debating it, but when I saw the redness in her eyes, I jumped up from my seat and stood in front of her.

"Cassidy, what's wrong?" I asked, gently holding her elbow to keep her from turning away from me.

"Nothing," she whispered, looking everywhere but at me.

"Bullshit. You've been crying. Why?"

"No, I haven't." Her voice was a low hiss as she looked around the table to see if anyone was listening to us.

A few other people joined us, leaving the only open seat for Cassidy next to me.

I took her glass of wine and set it down for her, still concerned with why she was upset.

"I'm going to go get food," she said, pulling away from me and heading for the buffet. Little did she know, she wasn't going to get away from me that easily.

I reached for her elbow again, smiling as we darted in between people and said hello as we got in line for the buffet.

"What's going on, Cassidy?" I asked again, my hand resting low on her back, trying to maintain a proper boundary so people didn't get the wrong idea.

"I told you, it's nothing." She tucked a strand of hair behind her ear and reached for a plate.

I followed her through the line, not bothering to pay attention to what I was putting on mine. Food was the least of my concerns right now. Cassidy was upset about something, and I was determined to find out what was wrong. Once we made our way through, I guided her back to the table and pulled out her seat for her.

Everyone was already engaged in conversation which made it easy for me to try to continue mine with Cassidy.

"You're really starting to worry me," I said softly, leaning in so I could keep my voice low.

"I'm fine. Really."

She picked up her fork and knife, cutting into her chicken as she made it clear that the conversation wasn't going to go any further.

Dinner was painfully long with not knowing what had Cassidy so upset when she first got there, but when she ordered a third glass of wine, I decided to put a stop to it. I knew she was staying at the hotel for the night, so she didn't have to worry about driving, but I still didn't want her trying to drink away whatever problem she was avoiding.

Melissa stood at the front of the room with Bruce while he gave a quick toast, thanking the employees for their hard work and dedication. I missed most of it, but I couldn't focus as I struggled to keep from reaching for Cassidy's hand underneath the table.

Everyone around us raised their glasses in the air and cheered. I lifted my water and absentmindedly clanked it against those around me. Melissa and Bruce worked on passing out the gifts, and I was surprised when I was handed the gift I had seen Cassidy come in with.

She held hers from me in her lap and played with the ribbon that I had tied around the box.

"You got me?" I asked, reading the tag again, just to make sure.

"Yeah. It's funny how that worked, huh? That out of all the employees at Waldon's, we would draw each other's names."

"Guess fate had plans for us."

She smiled, but it didn't reach her eyes or make them light up the way they looked when she was truly happy.

"You first," she said, nodding to the large box I was holding.

"Nope. Ladies first."

"Please?" It was the crack in her voice that killed me and made me open mine first.

Inside was a brand new ax, and I grinned, knowing Sam must have had a hand in this since he was the only one who knew mine was broken. In addition to the ax was a small box filled with some of my favorite snacks that we used to enjoy back when we were dating and would have our weekly movie night dates.

"Wow. Cass," I sighed, trying to focus on what I was trying to say while being so overcome with emotion. "Thank you. For all of this. I really appreciate it."

"I didn't know what to get you," she admitted, tapping her fingers along the top of the box she was holding on her lap. "I remembered how much you used to enjoy mixed nuts and Milk Duds back in the day, so I was hoping you still did."

"Well, you were right. It's still the perfect combination of salty and sweet. And thank you for the new ax. I actually needed one."

"My brother told me," she said, scrunching her nose in the most adorable way. "I'm sorry. I wanted to be a better gift giver, but I was coming up empty-handed."

"Don't be. These gifts are wonderful, Cassidy. I don't expect you to know what to give someone you haven't talked to in over a decade. People change. You know that."

"True, but I like to think that I *used* to know you better than anyone."

I didn't want to get into any heavy conversations right now because I wanted to have them when we could fully focus on them and not have the distraction of liquored-up coworkers. I let her comment go and nodded to her box.

"Your turn."

She smiled and pulled the ribbon off before lifting the lid and opening the box.

"Oh my God," she whispered, covering her mouth with both hands as she stared inside at the copy of *The Christmas Cabin* I had found for her. "How did you…"

She didn't have to complete her sentence for me to know what she was asking.

"I remembered you reading the book to me when we were younger, and then I overheard you and Rachel talking about it. I know it's not the same as the one your grandma gave you, but at least now you have a copy of it."

"Sean," she breathed, wiping the corners of her eyes. "This is the sweetest gift anyone has ever given me. Thank you so much."

"You're welcome." I smiled when she took it out of the box and slowly flipped the pages.

"I still can't believe you got one. How did you find it?" she asked softly, setting it back in the box.

"It took a little bit of work, but I got lucky."

"Why did you go through all of that when I've been treating you so terribly?"

I shrugged and looked down at the table, ignoring the look she was giving me.

"Of course." She lowered her head and shook it. "I should have known. I'm such an idiot."

She put the box on the table, then got up and rushed out of the room.

I followed after her, needing to know what was going on.

"Cassidy, wait," I called, rushing to catch up to her.

I grabbed her arm and spun her around to find tears spilling down her cheeks.

"What is going on?"

She wiped the tears away with the back of her hand and looked at me.

"Declan told me."

My body tensed at the mention of my brother.

"Told you what? When did you talk to him?"

"Earlier, when I came to check into my room. He was in the lobby with his wife, and she made him tell me about what happened back in high school. How it wasn't *you* that cheated on me. He was the one who cheated on his girlfriend but lied and said it was you."

She sobbed and covered her mouth as the tears continued to flow.

"Why didn't you tell me?" she asked, her body starting to tremble.

I scrubbed a hand down my face and stared at her.

"I tried. You didn't want to believe me."

"You should have tried harder," she cried, allowing me to pull her into my chest.

"I knew you wouldn't believe me until he came clean, Cassidy. And I didn't want to continue a relationship with you as long as you believed I had cheated on you because that thought would always be in the back of your mind, and it would taint whatever we had together."

"I can't believe I've hated you this entire time for something you didn't do."

She pulled away and wiped at her eyes.

"It's okay, Cass. I don't blame you for it."

"It's not okay, Sean. It's not okay that I've spent the last twelve years of my life hating you for something your brother did, yet you never stopped loving me. Don't you see that?"

I nodded, not sure what to say. She was right. I never stopped loving her, even when it killed me to see how much she hated me at times.

"For what it's worth, I'm sorry. I wish you would have known the truth sooner. But you're right, Cass. I've never stopped loving you, and I don't think I ever will."

"I love you too, Sean. Even when I tried to hate you, I still loved you."

She reached up and grabbed my face, pulling it to hers as our lips brushed against each other.

"I have a room," she murmured, her lips and face smushed against mine.

"Is that an invite?" I teased, grabbing a handful of her ass and squeezing.

"No. It's a demand." She pulled away, giving me a look that made me weak in the knees. "Come to my room with me so I can show you all the ways I love you and make up for hating you for so long."

I swallowed hard, my dick immediately hardening as her eyes darkened and she licked her lips.

Twenty-Eight
Cassidy

"Can I just say how beautiful you look tonight?" Sean said as he stood behind me and slowly kissed my neck, sending shivers along my skin.

We went back to the party to get our stuff and said our goodbyes, but neither of us wanted to spend longer in there than needed. We had a lot of time to make up for, and I wasn't about to waste a single second.

"Thank you. You know what would be even more beautiful?" My eyes fluttered as he moved to the other side of my neck.

"What's that?"

"Your dick buried deep inside of me."

He chuckled and made no effort to hurry as he continued kissing the spots he knew drove me crazy.

"I have been waiting what feels like a lifetime for this, Cass. I'm not going to rush tonight."

"Okay. I hear you. And I totally get where you're coming from," I said, already breathless again as he nipped at my ear. "But I'm going to explode and die a brutal death if you don't fuck me soon."

"I think you're being a little dramatic," he teased, pulling the thin strap of my dress down and kissing along my shoulder. "I just fucked you yesterday."

"I'm not dramatic. I'm horny, and you're delaying the orgasm I would kill for right now."

My eyes caught his as we stood facing the full-length mirror on the wall.

"Trust me, Cassidy. You're going to come. Multiple times. Until I decide you've had enough. Now stop complaining and allow yourself to enjoy what's happening." He gathered the fabric of my dress and slowly pulled it up, forcing the slit on the thigh up even higher.

"I would enjoy it more if your dick was—" I sucked in a breath and paused as he pushed my panties aside and slid a finger through my slit. "Ahhh! Fuck!"

"You're always so wet for me, baby. Such a good girl, ready to come for me."

I nodded, unable to get the words out, as he slid another finger in. I watched shamelessly in the mirror as he touched me.

"You like how I fuck you with my fingers, don't you?"

My head tipped back as my lips parted, but no words came out. It felt like my body was on fire from his touch, ready to explode into a puddle of bliss.

"I bet if I touched your clit, you'd come within seconds. Wouldn't you?"

"Yes," I breathed, already preparing myself for the delicious torture he was about to put me through.

He continued fucking me with two fingers as his thumb brushed against my clit, nearly sending me over the edge.

"Do you ever think about me when you play with yourself, Cass?" he asked, holding me against his body as he rubbed harder and faster.

"Yes!" I whimpered, my legs struggling to hold me up, my pussy spasming against his fingers as he drained every last bit of my orgasm out of me.

My eyes fluttered open as I tried to catch my breath, his strong arms holding me up.

"You're so fucking beautiful when you come."

"I love how easily you make me come," I replied as his fingers trailed softly over my skin as he slowly unzipped my dress, allowing it to fall to the floor at my feet.

He reached for my hand and helped me to step over it, wearing nothing but my matching black lace bra and panty set and black stiletto heels. His eyes brazenly roamed over my body, soaking in every tiny detail as he bit down on his hand to keep from touching me again.

"I can't wait to fuck you in that," he said, shaking his head as he let out a ragged breath.

I glanced down at his jeans, already noticing the prominent outline of his erection.

"Well, that will have to wait. I have something more pressing that's demanding my attention."

I took his hand and walked over to the floor-to-ceiling window, pulling the sheer curtains open.

I dropped to my knees, keeping my back against the window as I undid his jeans, sliding them down his legs along with his boxer briefs. His cock sprang free, jutting up to his stomach as a drop of precum glistened on the tip. I gripped it firmly in my hand as I looked up and locked eyes with him.

"Since I've called you Fucker Face for so long, it seems only fitting that I let you fuck my face," I teased, raising my eyebrows as I slowly wrapped my lips around him and took him to the back of my throat.

He closed his eyes and groaned as his hand grabbed the back of my head and held me steady. I flattened my tongue and played with his balls while sucking his dick. I could feel him tighten against me as I sucked harder, using my other hand to stroke what didn't fit in my mouth.

"Seriously, Cass, I'm going to come if you don't stop," he warned.

I pulled away, letting him pop out of my mouth as I wiped the corners and looked up at him while still holding his cock in my hand.

"I told you I was going to let you fuck my face, Sean. I meant it."

His eyes darkened as I took him back in my mouth, leaning in as I began bobbing up and down on his dick. I worked on relaxing my jaw as he hit the back of my throat, making my eyes tear up as I gagged a few times.

"Fuck," he growled.

I leaned back slightly, pulling him with me as I encouraged him to take over. His hand gripped the back of my head tighter as he began thrusting harder. I tilted my head slightly, allowing him to go deeper while I continued to stroke him.

He grunted, and his body tightened around me as I felt ropes of hot, salty cum hit the back of my throat. I continued sucking, making sure to get every drop before I allowed him to pull away. I wiped the corners of my mouth and grinned up at him as he stared down at me adoringly.

Twenty-Nine

Sean

She looked like a little minx, sitting there wiping her mouth as if she didn't just swallow a record-breaking amount of cum that I shot down her throat. I held out my hand and helped her up, already ready for another round with Cassidy.

"I don't want to know where you learned to do that," I whispered as I held her against my body. "But fuck, Cass. That was the hottest blow job I've ever had."

"Well, thank you. I hate to break it to you, but we're just getting started. I have lots of plans for you tonight."

"Lucky for you, I have all night and all day tomorrow."

"I thought you worked tomorrow?"

"Nope. I'm calling in sick. Fucked to death. It's a thing."

"I don't think Bruce will buy that as an excuse, nor will he care."

"I'll come up with something better then. But for now, I have plans for you," I teased, unhooking her bra in the back and pulling it off.

Her nipples puckered in the chilly room, and I wanted desperately to pull them into my mouth and suck them. I didn't want to rush things with her tonight, but I also found it nearly impossible to keep my hands to myself and not touch her.

I spun her around, having her face the window as I gently pushed her forward until her breasts were pressed against the glass.

"Fuck, that's cold," she hissed but made no effort to pull away.

I pulled my shirt off and tossed it to the floor, standing completely naked behind her as she wore nothing but her thong and those sexy heels.

"Spread your legs," I instructed, standing behind her as I guided her with my foot.

Her long legs spread to the side as I reached forward and slid my hand into her panties. It was a tight fit with how she was pressed against the window, but I didn't mind. The thought of someone watching me fuck her was so arousing that I got hard just thinking about it.

Knowing that she was wet and ready for me, I pulled my hand out of her panties and stroked myself before lining my dick up at her entrance. Just as I was about to push inside, I paused.

"Fuck. I need to grab a condom," I said, my aching dick painfully close to her warm, wet pussy.

"I'm on birth control," she offered, looking over her shoulder.

"I just did my physical and got tested. Nothing to report here."

"Same."

"Are you sure you want to do it without one?" I asked, not wanting to make her feel pressured to do anything.

"Yes," she said, pressing her ass against me in an invite.

I held my breath as I slowly pushed inside of her, closing my eyes as her tight pussy welcomed me.

"Ahhh," she moaned, letting her head fall back as her breasts pressed harder against the glass.

"Fuck, Cass," I breathed, moving slowly until she adjusted to me. "You make me want to fuck you hard against this window so everyone can see that you're mine."

"Do it." She spread her legs a little wider and pressed her ass up as I slid deeper inside of her. "Fuck me hard, Sean."

I placed one hand above hers on the window and lifted my hips as I began thrusting. I wrapped my other hand around her waist and held on as I fucked her hard and deep, getting harder as she moaned and gripped my cock with her pussy.

She lowered her hand into her panties and began rubbing her clit while I continued slamming into her from behind. I felt my balls tighten as I gripped her harder, holding onto her as I released my load deep inside of her as her pussy spasmed around me.

After we both took a moment to catch our breath, I wrapped her in my arms and held her.

"I can't believe I wasted twelve years missing out on that," she said sadly as she wrapped her arms around my neck and hugged me.

"It's okay. We have plenty of time to make up for the time we lost," I assured her as I lowered my mouth to hers and kissed her the way I'd been wanting to for years. I was going to spend the rest of the night taking my time making love to her.

Thirty
Cassidy

"You want me to read it again?" I said with a laugh as I leaned against Sean in the oversized garden tub.

We came in an hour ago to shower and clean up, but I convinced him to soak in a hot bath with me instead. We opened the bottle of wine I'd brought with me and the book he got me and cuddled up in the tub as I read to him. It felt like we were back in time, never having missed a beat from where we left off all those years ago.

"I like hearing your voice as you read," he replied, sighing contentedly.

"Well, then, how about we talk instead?"

"I like that idea too."

"I don't think there's much you *wouldn't* like right now," I teased, already feeling his cock hardening behind me.

"I'm relaxing in a hot bath with a naked girl who gives the best head I've ever gotten. What's *not* to like?"

"True. The only thing that would make this better would be freshly baked brownies with vanilla ice cream on top."

"I'll make you some when we go home?"

"Home?"

"Yep. I've decided that you're coming to stay with me for a bit until we get fucking each other every twenty minutes out of our system."

"That's all fun and good, but what are we supposed to do about Christmas? I don't think my family is going to take too kindly to me running outside to get my *stocking stuffed* if you know what I mean."

"That's easy, peasy. I'll come inside and say hi before taking you to your room to ravage you and get my fill."

"I don't think they're going to like that either," I said with a laugh. "But you are welcome to come have dinner with us if you're not busy."

My heart fluttered in my chest as worry started to wash over me. We weren't even technically back together—or at least we hadn't talked about whether we were or not. I couldn't just expect him to give up whatever plans he might have to join us.

"You don't have to. There's no pressure t—"

"I'll be there, Cass," he said, interrupting me as he held me tighter against him.

"Okay." My voice was barely above a whisper as I thought about how I was going to explain all of this to my family.

"Stop overthinking things," he warned, putting his hand on my thigh as my leg started to shake and the water sloshed over the side of the tub. "Everything will work out perfectly fine. I'll go to dinner with you at your parents' house if you come to lunch with me at my parents' house."

I turned my head to look at him, wondering if he was serious.

"You want me to come to your family's lunch?"

"I do. I think it would be nice having you there."

"What about Declan?"

"What about him?"

"I don't know," I rushed out, turning to face him the best I could. The tub was big, but it wasn't really big enough to turn around without someone losing a limb. "Don't you think things will be awkward between all of us after what happened?"

He shook his head, his answer evident on his face.

"Not at all. Eventually, we will all have to clear the air between us, and I think it's better to do it now instead of waiting and dragging it out. We're all adults. I don't see any reason to keep letting this come between us."

"That's easy for you to say," I replied with a soft laugh. "I'm still pretty angry with him for keeping us apart this whole time."

"Well, not to worry. I know just the thing to get that anger out of you."

He grabbed my arm and pulled me back to him, this time facing him as I straddled his lap.

"If this is how we're going to deal with my anger, I might have to keep finding new things to be mad about," I teased as I reached down and lined him up at my entrance.

He lifted his hips and pushed inside as I leaned forward and kissed him. We fit perfectly together, our bodies quickly becoming one as we made love.

Thirty-One
Cassidy

I rubbed my palms down the front of my dress, overly anxious about having lunch with Sean's family. It wasn't like I didn't know them; I used to hang out at their house all the time. But this time felt different.

I had told my parents and Sam this morning that Sean would be joining us for dinner. My mother squealed while my father smiled and hugged me. Sam wore a smug smile and reminded me that he told me so a while back. I punched him and then made my way out the door so I wasn't late for lunch.

When I pulled up in front of the house and parked, Sean was already outside waiting for me. He looked so handsome in his fitted sweater and dark jeans, with a smile that spread across his face as he came over to help me out of my car.

"You look beautiful," he said, pulling me into a warm hug as soon as I was out of the car.

"Thank you. You look very handsome."

"Thank you."

I pressed a soft kiss to his lips, then pulled away, my nerves skyrocketing.

"Relax. Everything is going to be fine," he said, taking the bottle of wine I'd brought and holding my hand as he led me to the front door.

Heavenly aromas floated through the air as we stepped inside. The house was beautifully decorated with garland and lights strung on the tree and Christmas music playing softly through the TV.

We walked through the living room and into the kitchen, where everyone was gathered and waiting for us. Just as I was about to panic from all of the attention being on me, his mom rushed over and wrapped me tightly in a hug. My body immediately relaxed as I hugged her back, missing this so much.

"Oh, Cassidy," she said softly before pulling back slightly and holding onto my hands as she studied my face. "It is so wonderful to have you join us today. Thank you for coming."

"Thank you for the invite," I replied with a smile.

She let me go as the two adorable girls I had met the other day came and pulled her away to show her something in the fridge. I said hello to Sean's dad before noticing that Declan and his wife were waiting for me.

"Hey," I said nervously, unsure of how to start. I felt Sean's hand rest on my lower back as Declan pulled his shoulders back and smiled at me.

"It's really wonderful to have you join us, Cassidy," Declan said, holding his wife's hand. "I just wanted to say again how sorry I am about everything. I didn't mean to upset you the other night, but I'm also glad that you now know the truth. I'm sorry I didn't tell you sooner. I messed things up for you and my brother, and I completely understand if neither of you forgive me for it. But please know that I do deeply regret what I did and how it impacted your relationship."

"Thank you. I appreciate that." I smiled and let out a heavy breath as they returned the smile before taking their seats at the table.

Sean guided me to where we were sitting and pulled out my chair. His dad sat at one end of the table and his mother at the other. The two little girls were seated on opposite sides, one right beside Sean and the other directly across from me. We all lowered our heads as his mother said grace.

I finally relaxed enough during lunch to enjoy it and found myself smiling more than I had in a really long time.

Thirty-Two
Sean

Lunch with Cassidy at my parents' house went better than I could ever have expected. I knew she was nervous about it. Hell, so was I. But just as I predicted, we were all able to move on from the past and act like civilized adults. By the time we left, Cassidy and Stephanie were exchanging phone numbers so they could keep in touch as the girls clung to Cassidy's side the entire time we were there.

I was thankful that my dad had a relatively good day and seemed present for most of it. On occasion, we would notice his memory would fail him, but he didn't let it frustrate him as much as it normally would.

We dropped my car off at my place and Cassidy drove us to her parents' house so we didn't have to take two cars since she was staying at my house tonight. I didn't want to rush through dinner with her family, but I also couldn't wait to have her to myself again. I wasn't just falling in love again; I was already in it and sinking fast.

"You ready?" Cassidy said as we walked up the driveway to the front door.

"More than ready. You?"

"It depends on how much eggnog they've already had. I never know what to expect with them," she teased as the door opened right as we got to it.

"Hello! Hello!" her mother said, stepping back so we could step inside. "Merry Christmas, you two!"

"Merry Christmas, Mom," Cassidy replied, leaning in to hug her. "Even though we've already done all of this when I was here this morning."

Amelia laughed and swatted at her daughter's shoulder.

"Merry Christmas," I said, hugging her mom. "Thank you for allowing me to join your family for dinner."

"Oh, dear. You're welcome anytime. We adore you and are so happy that you are here with us today."

I was thankful that her family did not seem to be holding any grudges or hard feelings about my so-called past infidelity. I didn't know if Cassidy had already told them about us or how it was Declan who had been caught cheating all those years ago. But none of that seemed to matter right now, so I wasn't going to waste my time or energy thinking about it.

We all sat down at the table, and I grinned seeing how many almost empty eggnog glasses there were sitting in front of her parents and Sam. Cassidy shook her head but couldn't stop the corners of her lips from turning up into a smile.

"Would you like some eggnog?" Sam offered, holding up the pitcher as he refilled the other glasses.

I looked at Cassidy, hoping she would give me some guidance.

"He'll have some," she answered for me with a flirty smirk.

"I'm driving tonight so none for me."

"It's not Christmas without a little eggnog," her mother interjected. "I have some that's not spiked. Do you want some of that instead?"

"Sure. That sounds wonderful."

The girls went to the fridge and talked quietly while I sat at the table with her dad and brother, who were both staring strangely at me.

"If you hurt her, I will poison your coffee and make it look like an accident," Sam said with a grin that made it look like he'd just told me how much he loves puppies.

"And I know how to dispose of a body without anyone realizing it's missing," her father added with his fingers steepled in front of him.

"Umm—" I started, snapping my mouth closed as I struggled with how to respond to that.

Just then, they both burst into laughter, nudging each other with their elbows.

"We're just fucking with you," Sam said, shaking his head that I fell for it.

"Whew," I replied, letting the air in my lungs out in a long, heavy breath. "Not gonna lie, I was a bit worried there for a minute."

"Don't be. We both know that if you do anything to fuck things up with Cassidy, she'll kick your ass herself," Sam confirmed, his dad nodding his head in agreement.

"Whose ass am I kicking?" Cassidy said as she and her mother returned to the table and sat down.

"No one." I leaned in and kissed her cheek, feeling everyone's eyes on us.

But that wasn't a lie because I would go to my last day making sure I never hurt her again.

Thirty-Three
Cassidy

"Hello! I missed you, too," I said, rubbing the top of Max's head as he jumped up and held onto me the best he could the second I walked into the house.

"Traitor," Sean teased, shaking his head at his dog, who was obsessively following me into the living room while Sean worked on bringing our stuff in from the car.

"He's not a traitor. He just loves me. You can't blame him for that."

"No. You're right. I can't blame him for that, but I can be jealous of him trying to steal you away from me."

"Trust me, you have nothing to worry about. I love you both equally."

"Ouch," he said, holding a hand to his chest as if I'd hurt him. "I was kinda hoping that you would love me more than him."

"I don't want to hurt his feelings," I whispered while covering his cute little ears with my hands.

"I would say you won't, but he's seriously the most emotional and needy dog I've ever met."

I laughed and gave Max another head scratch before going

to the kitchen, where Sean was putting the leftovers my mom sent with us in the fridge. It had been a long—but fun—day and I was ready to just sit down and relax. It felt weird not having a gift for Sean, but it wasn't like we expected to get back together a few days before Christmas.

"So, what do you want to do tonight?" he asked, wrapping his arms around my waist and kissing my neck.

I let out a soft moan and closed my eyes as he grabbed a handful of my ass.

"This," I whispered.

"Make out in my kitchen?" he teased.

"As long as it leads to you fucking me, then yes."

"Such a naughty mouth."

"And I know exactly what to do with it." I opened my eyes and looked up at him, batting them.

"Is that my next gift?" he asked, his eyes darkening as his voice deepened.

"Well, you know how I like to give the gift that keeps on giving."

I winked and chewed my lower lip, giggling when he picked me up and carried me to his bedroom caveman style. Things with Sean had been strained for so long, but now that all of that was in the past, it was time for us to move forward and celebrate our love for each other.

****

If you'd like to hang out and chat books, be sure to find me in my reader group on Facebook! I would love to have you in there!

https://www.facebook.com/groups/2945710968775398/

Ready for more steamy holiday romance? Be sure to check out the rest of the Sugarplum Falls series!

Blame It On The Mistletoe
https://books2read.com/u/bw1rqe
Blame It On The Eggnog
https://books2read.com/u/38PPY6
Blame It On The Candy Canes
https://books2read.com/u/31DNo7
Blame It On The Blizzard
https://books2read.com/u/b6z6XE
Blame It On The Reindeer
https://books2read.com/u/baLAG6
Blame It On The Carols
https://books2read.com/u/me8E9z
Blame It On The Lattes
https://books2read.com/u/mB1E2A

Other Books By Samantha Baca
The Haven Brook Series
(small-town romantic suspense):

'Til Death Do Us Part (Haven Brook Book 1)

https://books2read.com/u/m2RJNR

The Cradle Will Fall (Haven Brook Book 2)

https://books2read.com/u/b6O0QE

The Ties That Bind (Haven Brook Book 3)

https://books2read.com/u/mqgoz8

A Very Haven Christmas (Haven Brook Book 4- Novella)

https://books2read.com/u/mvqGjj

Three Strikes, You're Gone (Haven Brook Book 5)

https://books2read.com/u/mvqL2z

<u>The Dark Shadows Trilogy</u>
<u>(romantic suspense)</u>

Five Steps Ahead (Dark Shadows Book 1)

https://books2read.com/u/38Q0gO

Ten Seconds Too Late (Dark Shadows Book 2)

https://books2read.com/u/3JRgVB

Against The Clock (Dark Shadows Book 3)

https://books2read.com/u/m2YwoR

<u>The Stone Creek Series</u>
<u>(small-town- novellas)</u>

Chocolate Covered Mistletoe (Stone Creek Book 1)

https://books2read.com/u/3LRk9N

Candy Coated Promises (Stone Creek Book 2)

https://books2read.com/u/mldP5Y

Pumpkin Spiced Possibilities (Stone Creek Book 3)

https://books2read.com/u/bojdwV

Beaumont Creek Series
(small town)

Just One Time (Beaumont Creek Book 1)

https://books2read.com/u/3G52zK

Second Chances (Beaumont Creek Book 2)

https://books2read.com/u/4Aj6Z0

Third Time's The Charm (Beaumont Creek Book 3)

https://books2read.com/u/b5lEyG

Four-ever Single (Beaumont Creek Book 4)

https://books2read.com/u/4j5jMX

Fifth Wheel (Beaumont Creek Book 5)

https://books2read.com/u/4XwKwa

<u>Whiskey Mountain Series</u>
<u>(small-town- novellas)</u>

Something To Talk About

https://books2read.com/u/4X62ag

Something To Think About

https://books2read.com/u/3GWAan

Something To Believe In

https://books2read.com/u/3yVzgB

Something To Live For

https://books2read.com/u/mllEOP

<u>Sugarplum Falls Series</u>
<u>(Holiday Novellas- can be read as standalone)</u>

Blame It On The Mistletoe
https://books2read.com/u/bw1rqe

Blame It On The Eggnog
https://books2read.com/u/38PPY6

Blame It On The Candy Canes
https://books2read.com/u/31DNo7
Blame It On The Blizzard
https://books2read.com/u/b6z6XE

Blame It On The Reindeer
https://books2read.com/u/baLAG6

Blame It On The Carols
https://books2read.com/u/me8E9z

Blame It On The Lattes
https://books2read.com/u/mB1E2A

Blame It On The Secret Santa
https://books2read.com/u/mY9dGY

<u>Standalone Books</u>

One Last Wish

https://books2read.com/u/mqg7D9

Finding Love In Apartment 2C (novella)

https://books2read.com/u/bze9aZ

Cocky Counsel: A Hero Club Novel

https://books2read.com/u/31Kzkn

All Is Fair In Food And War (novella)

https://books2read.com/u/bp8qjX

<u>Holiday Books</u>
<u>(novellas)</u>

Snow Place To Go

https://books2read.com/u/4A560N

A Very Merry Kissmas

https://books2read.com/u/bPDgy7

A Christmas Wish

https://books2read.com/u/4EKXpE

Holiday Hijinks

https://books2read.com/u/4DP6Ze

Acknowledgments

When I was a little girl, I had a dream of being an author one day. I wanted to sit in a cabin in Colorado and watch the snow fall as I wrote stories people would love. While I might not live in Colorado, and I rarely get to see snow, I have accomplished my childhood dream of being a published author and writing stories people love.

Fast forward to April 2020, when I nervously released my debut novel into the world, not knowing what would happen next. I thought for sure it was a one-and-done thing, but then I realized that the vault I had secretly been keeping stories locked up inside of had been unlocked, and there was no stopping me from that point on.

It's wild to think that Blame It On The Secret Santa is the 36th book I have written and published. It blows my mind how many books I publish every year and how far I've gone with something that started as just a fun hobby. Now, I can truly say that this is what I do for a living, and even though I work harder than I have with any other job, this one is absolutely the most fulfilling.

None of this would be possible without the help and support of so many people. I have a wonderful team of alpha readers, as well as an incredible team of beta readers. Between them, they help me polish each book and make it the best it can be.

Azucena, Amanda, Valerie, and Claire—thank you, ladies, for all of your help, especially when this book became so frustrating for me. Thanks for talking me off the ledge and keeping me from putting this one in the trash and calling it a day. You're so supportive of everything in my life, and I'm thankful for each of you and our friendships!

Malissa, Tamara, Jackie, and Karrie—you ladies always show up for me, and your support has been constant and unwavering from the beginning. I appreciate all of your feedback and suggestions for things that we missed during the first round. I'm thankful for you ladies and our friendships as well!

I don't think I have a single book with an acknowledgment section that doesn't have the words *as always,* so let's throw that in!

As always, I want to give a huge thank you and shout out to my ARC readers for always helping to spread the word about my new releases and for giving their honest opinions about my books in their reviews. I'd also like to thank the readers who pick up one of my books and give them a try! Without readers who enjoy my books, I wouldn't have a reason to keep doing what I do.

My parents and sister continue to be some of my biggest cheerleaders and have always supported me since I was a child. Thank you for always encouraging me when things get hard and for so proudly telling people that your daughter/sister is an author. I love you guys so much!

This may be my 36th book acknowledgment, but I absolutely, positively wouldn't be able to do any of this without my incredibly generous and talented husband. Not only does he help with my covers and the formatting of my books, but he never stops supporting me. I love to see the smile on his face when he talks about how far I've come with my publishing career and the things we have lined up for the future. I love you so much, my love. Thank you for everything you do!

And last but certainly not least, I want to thank my sweet girls for their support and for loving that mommy writes books. My heart warms at how much you both enjoy reading and how you've both mentioned wanting to be authors when you grow up as well. I hope that the creativity that you have inside of you brings you so much happiness as you explore what you want to do in life. The sky is the limit, and I'll be there every step of the way to help you get closer to your goals.

If you'd like to hang out and get to know me better, I'm super active in my reader group on Facebook. I also do frequent newsletters with sales and freebies when I have them, so be sure to sign up for those if you'd like to. You can find me at www.samanthabaca.com. From the menu, you can find a handful of bonus content, as well as a page with links for all of my social media.

About the Author

Samantha lives in the southwest with her husband and two small children after abandoning her childhood dream of living in a cabin in Colorado when she found that she couldn't afford to live there and was deathly allergic to the woods. When she's not writing, she's usually spouting off sarcastic remarks while drinking wine out of a coffee mug to look like a functional adult while chasing down her toddlers. She enjoys spending time with her family, watching reruns of Friends, and the 24/7 flow of coffee that can be found in her veins. Be sure to follow her on social media for updates on what she's working on.

You can find her here:

Facebook: https://www.facebook.com/AuthorSamanthaBaca

Instagram: https://instagram.com/author_samantha_baca

Goodreads: http://www.goodreads.com/authorsamanthabaca

Facebook Reader Group: https://www.facebook.com/groups/2945710968775398/

Webpage: www.samanthabaca.com

Newsletter: http://eepurl.com/g0NcSj

www.ingramcontent.com/pod-product-compliance
Lightning Source LLC
Chambersburg PA
CBHW020656010826
48969CB00013B/2169